THE LONG DARK

A Jake Sawyer novella

ANDREW LOWE

I hold a beast, an angel, and a madman in me.

—Dylan Thomas

Prologue

The woman crawled along the edge of the road, bare knees scraping across the warm asphalt.

She hauled her limbs up and over the high kerb, one by one, slapping them down on the pavement.

The baby kicked in her belly; a silent rebuke.

She overbalanced and rolled onto her back, then stared up at the night sky: deep, deep black.

Glistening lone stars, scattered clusters, luminous nebulae sculpted by gas and dust.

Behind the bruises and swollen skin, her eyes feasted on the cosmic lightshow: alive on her retinas in the here and now, dead at source.

'¡Señora!'

A shout from the petrol station across the road.

Male, but not one of them.

She took a breath, then righted herself on all fours. Groaning with every movement, chasing every breath.

Blood dripped from her broken nose, spotting and

puddling onto the stone. Like ink under the pale streetlamp.

'*¿Estás bien?*'

She raised her head. Further up the pavement, a single-storey house sat in the centre of a small garden, surrounded by a low stone wall.

No lights on in the house. Cluttered shadows in the garden. Trees or plants?

If she could make it to the wall, she could rest against it.

The pavement inclined, steepening as it swerved to a huddle of white stone houses at the edge of Teguise.

The old capital, asleep at this hour.

If she could make it to the wall, she could turn and see who was calling her. She could check herself over, answer his question.

Another kick in her belly. More like a prod.

She crawled on, crossing the pavement, loose T-shirt dusting the ground. Knees scraping again; no energy to lift them, but she was numb to pain.

At the wall, she leaned a shoulder into the volcanic rock and planted her fingers at the top, pulling herself up, raising her head for a closer look at the garden.

The shadows were home-made statues and figurines rendered in clay and plaster, crowded around pillars of cacti. Leering goblins, scowling warriors, vogueing deities.

It was a chaos of cultures, religions, ethnicities, art styles, deliciously corrupted by random pop culture plastics: dolls' heads, toy cars, TV sets.

A permanent exhibition of outsider art in the centre of an island spat out by a volcano fifteen million years earlier.

The spectacle made the woman's head swim, and she

slumped to the side, caught by the man from the petrol station.

'*Señora. ¿Qué pasó?*'

Another man arrived. They carefully turned her back to the wall and crouched either side, keeping her upright.

Her head drooped, and blood from her nose flowed onto her lips, into her mouth.

The second man leaned in close, trying to make eye contact. She smelt tobacco, hair oil, unbrushed teeth.

He held her shoulders. '*Inglesa?* What happened? Who has done this?'

The first man stood up and made a phone call. He paced, shouting into the phone. '*¡Ambulancia!*'

The woman's head fell back, and she refocused on the night sky, her eyelids dropping.

The stars going out.

'*¡Sí, sí! ¡Rápido! ¡Policía!*'

Chapter One

'Other worlds are possible.'

'Sorry?' Sheena Harley slid her bare feet down from the dashboard and looked up from her phone.

'Written across the bridge we just passed.'

'Didn't see it.'

Jake Sawyer glanced over from the driver seat, green eyes flashing in the sun flare off the windscreen. '*Otros mundos son posibles.*'

'*Buen, señor.*' Harley reached over, ran her long fingers down his cheek, tracing the edge of the dimple. 'Do you believe that?'

He shrugged. 'Well, it's more poetic than the graffiti on the Roach Point Bridge.'

'*Fuck the police?*'

'Yeah.'

'You'd think the police would get that cleaned.'

Sawyer floored it past a minivan loaded with bikes and surf gear. 'We *are* the police.'

'Well, I'm certainly not cleaning it.'

'Your talents lie in other directions.'

Harley took off her Gucci sunglasses and hitched her streaked blonde hair into a ponytail. She propped her feet back up on the dash, adjusted the sun visor mirror and swiped sunscreen onto her nose and forehead.

Sawyer glanced over again. 'You're waiting.'

'Yeah. For the dig about community policing. Something about how I'm not real police?'

'You're prevention, I'm cure. Both needed. Both real.' He reached over to the glovebox.

Harley slapped his hand away and opened it herself. She pulled out a packet of wine gums and rummaged through it. 'You're out of red.'

'Black, then.'

Sawyer opened his mouth, keeping his eyes on the road.

Harley slipped the sweet onto his tongue and turned to her window, gazing out at the rippling fields of basaltic ash that flowed west to the UNESCO mountain range.

'Timanfaya,' said Harley, pointing.

He side-eyed. 'Been on Trip Advisor?'

She shoved him.

'It means *fire mountain*,' said Sawyer.

'Ah! Not quite. I did some research.'

Another side-eye. 'Googled it.'

A harder shove. 'They don't actually know where the word comes from. Apparently, it's something to do with the people who lived here before the Spanish claimed it.'

'The Guanches. North African Berbers.'

Harley rolled her eyes, turned back to the window. 'Smart arse.'

'I can work the internet, too, you know.'

Harley shrugged, sulky. 'They have camels at Timanfaya.'

'Yeah. For the tourists.'

'We're tourists.'

Sawyer sped past a low-rise whitewashed building with an oversized sign over the entrance doors: *MUSEUM*.

'Let's go there,' said Harley. 'It says, *ENTRADA GRATIS*.'

Sawyer kept his eyes on the road. 'It's free because it's essentially a shop.'

'It's an aloe vera museum. *The aloe vera plant is well-suited to the arid, subtropical climate. It provides ample sunlight, mild temperatures and well-drained soil—*'

Sawyer grinned, made a grab for her phone. She pulled it away and carried on reading. *'The volcanic soil of Lanzarote, rich in minerals, contributes to the healthy growth of—'*

'Okay, okay. I need a steer. Look up Mirador del Río.'

'I thought you knew where you were going.'

'Roughly, yes. But I'm not a carrier pigeon.'

Harley set up the destination in the car satnav and sat back in her seat, staring out of the window again. 'This place is weird. There's no green.'

'Greener than Hackney.'

'Yeah. Between all the black and ash. It's like someone set fire to the place.'

'That's exactly what happened.'

She gasped in mock shock and twisted round to face him, eyes wide. 'If we go to this volcano place tomorrow, is there a chance something will erupt?'

'Is that a euphemism?'

She snorted and folded her legs beneath her. 'Something geological.'

'No chance. Nothing since 1824.'

Harley rested the side of her head against the seat and stared up at Sawyer. 'I like you.'

'Thank fuck for that.'

'You're like the cool one in the band. Not the lead singer or guitarist. Not the obvious one, but the one everyone secretly fancies.'

Sawyer laughed. 'Can you give me any examples?'

She thought for a moment. 'Drummer out of Duran Duran.'

'Not Roger Taylor—'

'Yes!'

'Wasn't he in Queen?'

Harley turned back to the window. 'Different Roger Taylor.' She sighed and they were silent for a moment, listening to the music: undulating drone guitar, sweet and sinister female vocals. 'Can we change this? Bit intense.'

'Intense? It's my—'

She held up a hand. 'I know it's your favourite album. I like it, but it's zoning me out.' She connected her phone to the sound system. The music switched to a pulsing beat with a cycling synth melody. It built to a crescendo, then dropped out to a female vocal. 'This is similar. Just a bit more poppy.'

Sawyer shook his head. 'Crystal Castles is not similar to My Bloody Valentine.'

'You complain when I play 1980s music. I complain when you play 1990s music. Compromise. This is 2000s.' She hitched her legs up onto the dash again and stared out of the window. 'We could have gone to Paris, Jake. Or the Amalfi Coast.'

'Everyone goes there. That's why we're here.'

'Everyone goes there because it's beautiful. The food

is amazing. The views...' She waved a hand at the window and wrinkled her nose.

'You don't think this is beautiful?'

'In its own way, I suppose. But it's more...'

He grinned at her. 'Weird? Doesn't this feel more like an adventure, though? We're just off the tip of Africa. They've made films here. *One Million Years BC.* This is the birthplace of *Krull*, for Christ's sake.'

'It's... interesting. But not romantic.'

'That sounds like a challenge.' Sawyer glanced over.

Harley didn't look, but he could tell she was smiling.

Chapter Two

'This is insane,' said Harley.

She ran her hand along the milky white wall, which seemed to flow up to the ceiling, integrated into the rock. Organic shapes, undulating lines.

'It's like 1970s Stanley Kubrick made a Bond movie,' said Sawyer.

'And this is where the villain would live.'

'Exactly.'

'Despite all the local volcanoes.'

They crossed the dark-wood floor, past upscale diners, beneath a vast wrought-iron artwork: an abstract chandelier of birds and fish suspended on slender rods.

Light music; jazzy but not too hectic.

Fern-like plants hung from the ceiling corners, their tendrils free to waft against the walls, caress the floor. Potted versions, flared like candelabras, flanked the entrances to private cubicles.

They stepped out of the café onto a balustraded viewing platform.

'It is *hot*,' said Harley.

The North Atlantic lay before them under a pure cobalt sky. Small boats drifted by, unhurried, leaving trails like slow-motion comets.

Sawyer climbed a raised patch of petrified rock and shielded his eyes from the sun. 'I think it was an old military base. Then it was redesigned by a local artist in the 1970s.'

Harley looked up at him. 'César Manrique. I've read the Wikipedia page, too.'

He ignored her. 'I like the way it's built into the rock rather than plonked on top of it. Blending art and nature, making it hard to see from the outside.'

Harley stood behind Sawyer and put her arms around his waist. 'Camouflage.'

He turned. 'Huh?'

'I think that's the word you're looking for.' She whispered, conspiratorial. 'Blending in. Masking your true nature.' She raised her voice again. 'And this…' She swept her arm across the view, then ducked into a patch of shade. 'This is the Strait of El Río. Christ. It's *too* hot.'

Sawyer pointed to the detached land mass off to the north. 'So, what's that?'

She spun, headed back inside. 'An island.'

SPECIAL_IMAGE-OEBPS/images/break-rule-screen.svg-REPLACE_ME

'Any fallout from the trafficking raid?' Harley twisted spaghetti round her fork.

Sawyer shrugged. 'The AFO was fine in the end. I apologised for screwing up. He accepted. The boss is still sulking, but he'll get over it soon.'

'I've heard Hatfield is a bit of a nightmare.'

Sawyer unwrapped his panini, moved in for a bite.

'He's unreconstructed, but you don't get to DCI unless you've got something about you.'

'And you got the bastards? The Romanians.'

He looked out of the window, watched a couple take a joint selfie on the balcony. She smiled; he didn't. 'Yeah. We got the bastards.'

Harley leaned forward, jangling her bracelets. 'You've never told me the full story.'

'You don't want to know.'

She stroked his hand. 'Come on, Jake. The most excitement I've had recently was handing out a fixed penalty for a breach on a dog control order.'

Sawyer sighed and took a slug of Orangina from the bottle. 'You know most of it. Young woman murdered at a sex party in Radlett. Strangled. Hatfield put me on it, along with another DI, Max Reeves. It was a private house, and we found out they were making amateur porn there. The owner claimed the death was rough sex gone wrong.'

'And was it?'

Sawyer chomped off a corner of the panini. 'It was. But the porn was financed by a Romanian OCG, and the performers were trafficked from Eastern Europe.'

Harley pointed. 'And the victim's history blew open the trafficking ring.'

He nodded. 'The joy of victimology. Sometimes you get a different story than the one you expect. But there was a complication. We got access to their client list. Reeves was a regular at the party, with his girlfriend.' Harley squinted, confused. 'His wife didn't know.'

'Ouch. So the investigation pulled out his name?'

'Yeah. I stupidly tried to cover it up, but Hatfield sniffed it out. It wasn't relevant to the investigation, and I was just trying to keep Reeves's marriage together, but Hatfield hit the roof. Like I say, he's still up there.'

Harley sprinkled dressing over her salad. 'So, what happened on the raid?'

He chewed for a while. 'I had a moment.'

Harley raised her eyebrows, waiting for more.

'The Romanians were expecting us,' continued Sawyer. 'Probably a tip-off from the party owner. Reeves and I went in with the assault team. I checked over a room but missed a bad guy hiding in a closet. He jumped the AFO. Nearly got his rifle off him.'

'And the AFO was stabbed?'

Sawyer nodded, put down the panini. 'Reeves offered to cover for me, but I took it on the chin and wrote the report myself.'

'And did Hatfield insist you take this break?'

'No. I did. I needed to refocus.'

'And how's that going?' She shovelled in a weighty parcel of spaghetti and salad.

Sawyer didn't answer. He sipped his drink, watched the couple embrace. She had long black hair. Glossy. He looked away. 'Did you see the dome-like building up high on the way in?'

'Where?'

'On the twisty road as we drove up and out of Haría. It's an observation point. The highest spot on the island. Great for stargazing.'

Harley slapped her hands down on the table. 'Oh! Let's do that. I can educate you on the constellations. My brother and I had a telescope when we were little. Daddy's company made them, among other things.'

'Can I help you guys with anything else?'

They turned to the waiter, poised at the table. Neat black beard, man bun.

'Yes,' said Harley, leaning forward on her elbows. 'Is it normally this hot here?'

'No. *Calima* is coming soon.'

'What's that?' said Sawyer.

The waiter searched for the words. 'It's a sandstorm. It comes in from the Sahara sometimes. Always in summer. From Africa. It can get very dusty and hot.' He shrugged. 'I can feel it coming now. How long are you staying?'

'Five days,' said Harley.

He winced. 'If you're lucky, you'll get to see it. If you're unlucky, it will delay your flight. Because of…' He thought for a moment. 'Visibility.'

'Thanks,' said Sawyer. 'Your English is better than my Spanish.'

'*Gracias*.' He headed off.

'*Señor*.' Harley sprung to her feet. '*¿Dónde está el baño?*'

The waiter pointed to a corner near the bar.

Harley winked at Sawyer. 'Need the loo.'

Sawyer walked back out onto the balcony. The couple had climbed to a higher outcrop of rock. The black-haired woman gazed out to sea while the man rubbed sunscreen over her upper back.

She tossed her head and swished her hair forward over her shoulder.

Sawyer felt the swell in his stomach and ducked into shade. But it was too late.

Even here?

The view dropped out and he was down on the verge. Knees in the soil.

His brother, groaning and sobbing.

Their dog, barking in pain and fear.

He crawled, through the blood-spattered grass, with a screaming headache. Blinded by the low afternoon sun.

The hammer, rising and falling.

Metal into bone.

Above, the black-haired woman shrieked with laughter, jolting him back into the moment.

Sawyer took out his phone and navigated to an image: a pap shot of a short man getting into a police car. He zoomed in on his face. He was early fifties, worried-looking, with a rich crop of salt-and-pepper hair, centre-parted.

The head was down, eyes fixed on the floor.

'Six hundred and seventy metres.'

He startled, turned to find Harley behind him. 'What is?'

'Peñas del Chache. The highest point on Lanzarote. We have to go one night.' She pointed to Sawyer's phone. 'Who's this?'

'Someone who's been in prison for a long time and is about to get out.'

She draped her arms over Sawyer's shoulders. 'How long?'

'Almost thirty years.'

Harley whistled. 'So, he did a bad, bad thing.' She turned to the sea, inhaled deeply. 'Imagine being stuck away like that. Not being able to see this. Whoever you are, whatever you've done, it must be soul-destroying to be shut off from everything for so long.'

Sawyer turned back into the light, slid on his sunglasses. 'Particularly when you're innocent.'

Chapter Three

Sawyer climbed down the uneven rocky steps, barefoot and topless. He took a lounger in the shade beneath a cluster of tall palms with manicured trunks and set down his paperbacks and glass of Diet Coke on the mosaic tiles.

An early evening breeze rippled the surface of the solar-heated pool and Sawyer looked up to the verdant landscaped gardens integrated into the grounds. Their estate hotel, Casa Tomarén, was an old farm in the centre of the island, converted into rustic villas and suites. The location was unfashionable, but, like its host island, the sleepiness was part of the charm.

He gazed across the surrounding scrubby plain to the village of Mozaga, its whitewashed buildings swallowed in shadow from the setting sun.

'True to his own spirit.'

Sawyer turned to see a middle-aged woman sitting upright on the edge of her lounger, smiling.

She pointed to his back. 'Your tattoo.'

'You speak Greek?'

The woman laughed. 'I *am* Greek. I'm from Rhodes. Another island.' She gave an exaggerated shrug. 'What can I say? I'm happy when I'm fortified. By water.' She held up a capacious glass filled with pink liquid. 'And other delights. I'm Katerina.'

'Jake.'

She smiled and took a drink. 'What are you reading, Jake?'

Sawyer held up both books: *Tinker, Tailor, Soldier, Spy* and *The Outsider*. 'Comfort and a challenge.'

'Which is which?'

'I've tried with le Carré but always struggled. It'll click one day.'

Katerina sat up further. 'So, Camus is your comfort? Goodness. I only read chick lit on holiday. Pure fluff. I can't cope with anything reflective when it's this hot. I've always wanted a tattoo but I'm too squeamish about needles. Tell me about yours.'

On the other side of the pool, a younger woman in a pink-and-white bikini rose from her lounger and padded down the stone path to an open communal shower. She stood beneath the water, rubbing shampoo into her mid-length black hair.

'Is it a quote? *Kata ton daimona eautou*?'

'Sort of. It's from Jim Morrison's grave in Paris. His father chose it. I visited it when I was a teenager.'

Katerina beamed, nodding vigorously. 'And it spoke to you.'

'Yes. My mum… She loved The Doors. Lots of sixties guitar music. Usually the darker stuff. Hendrix, Cream, Velvet Underground.'

'So, it's a tribute to your mother.'

'It is. She died quite young.'

She put down her drink and frowned. 'I'm sorry to hear that, Jake.'

'Thank you.'

'My mother is still with us. I'm not sure she's too aware of the fact, but...' She shrugged. 'You know, though, that *daimona* can translate to *demon* as well as *spirit?* In the New Testament sense, that's *daimon* as a *demon that possesses.*'

'My girlfriend has pointed this out, yes. She's a polyglot. Greek, Spanish, Italian, French.'

Katerina took a drink. 'My God. That's so impressive. How do people do that?'

'Jake!' A call from their studio cottage around the back of the pool.

'Is that her?' said Katerina.

Sawyer got up. 'Yes. I've been summoned.'

'Come and see this!'

'Nice to meet you, Jake.' Katerina raised her glass. 'It's a good tattoo.'

He got up and headed for the steps. 'Thanks. Maybe a bit earnest. I was young.'

Katerina waved a hand. 'We were all young once.' She looked across at the man sleeping in the lounger beside her: hairy, egg-shaped. 'Although with some people, it's hard to believe.'

SPECIAL_IMAGE-OEBPS/images/break-rule-screen.svg-REPLACE_ME

Sawyer flopped onto the bed beside Harley. The mattress was too springy, and his weight bounced her up, a couple of inches clear of the bed.

'Jesus!' She shoved him.

'Sorry. What am I seeing?'

A small, wall-mounted TV looked down on the bed,

babbling in Spanish. The screen showed a sharp-suited man with a grey goatee standing before a giant backdrop of live footage. Headlines scrolled across the bottom.

'TV Canaria,' said Harley. 'Local news.'

The screen split to show a woman holding a branded mic, poised for a camera piece. The shot pulled back slowly as she spoke, revealing her position beside a white building at the top of a sloping main road that stretched into the far distance, flanked by empty plains.

The man turned to camera, animated and gesticulating.

'Is there an English version?' said Sawyer.

Harley gave him a look.

On-screen, the man spoke into camera, addressing the woman. She nodded and replied.

Harley held up a hand. 'She's saying that a young woman is being cared for after a couple of locals found her collapsed on the roadside.' She reached across and put the hand on his arm. 'She was five months pregnant.'

'Where is this?'

'Teguise. It's a town not far from here.'

Sawyer watched and listened, trying to pick up words he recognised. 'How is the woman now?'

'She was badly beaten... lost a lot of blood... and... Oh, Jesus. She miscarried. Poor woman.'

'ID?'

Harley listened. 'They're appealing for witnesses... They want to know how she got there. *Afirma que la mujer... Para ayudar...* The reporter says police are hoping to release pictures soon to help identify her.'

Chapter Four

Harley tore away a ragged chunk of pizza, taking care not to break any of her long coral-pink fingernails. 'Don't they do triangles here?'

Sawyer propped his feet on the veranda table. 'It's *good*.'

'No, it's not. It's okay.' She inspected the takeaway box. 'And this is barely cardboard.'

'You should go on *I'm A Celebrity... Get Me Out Of Here!*'

She scoffed. 'I suppose I should be thankful they even have pizza.'

Sawyer ran a hand along her outer thigh: smooth and warm. 'We'll eat out tomorrow. Somewhere more civilised for you.'

The sky over the plain had faded from bruised purple to shadowy brown to coal-black. Silhouettes of shrub foregrounded the sparse stone houses at the village edge, now twinkling with light from their integrated windows.

'They call the locals Canarians,' said Harley.

'Snappier than Lanzaroteans.'

'And they're Spanish citizens.'

Sawyer nodded. 'Technically.'

She slumped, petulant. 'It's so empty. Nothing going on.'

'You say that like it's a bad thing.' He pulled away an elastic string of cheese, threaded it into his mouth. 'Some people like nothing going on. The simple life. Plato said, "The good life is a life of virtue."'

She waved a hand, flopped back, took a big drink of wine. 'Still hot. And don't tell me I should be drinking water, not wine. I'm on holiday.'

He smiled. 'Therefore, you're obligated to drink wine?'

'Yes. I can't drink wine at home in London. I mean, I can. But it feels wrong. You're supposed to indulge when you're on holiday. You should feel free.'

'I like the idea that a spacious flat in Stamford Hill is somehow stifling.'

'Oh!' Harley clinked down her wine and edged her chair closer to Sawyer. 'Daddy wants to sell the flat. But don't worry. He's willing to contribute to something more *me*. Maybe even a house.'

Sawyer chewed on a crust, nodding. 'He wants you to get married.'

Harley laughed. 'What?'

'It's for your mum. It would legitimise us in her eyes. A bigger place would be his cue. He'll give it a few weeks then gently raise the subject. He might even feed you a line about tiny pattering feet.'

'Oh, fuck off, Jake. You make Mummy sound like some kind of religious maniac. You marrying me wouldn't change you, would it? She can't make you Jewish.'

'I'm sure she'd love to try.'

She laughed, harder. 'Talking of religious maniacs, didn't you say your father had heard the Good News?'

'That was ages ago. And he has an excuse.'

Harley sipped her wine, looked out to the plain.

Here it comes.

'I'd still love to hear more about your mum, Jake.'

Sawyer replied by tearing off a strip of pizza. He ate it slowly.

Harley stared into her glass. 'Anyway...' She reached over and relieved him of the pizza, tossing it into the open box. 'Plenty of time before we have to worry about all that.' She eased off her chair and climbed onto Sawyer, straddling him, digging her fingers through his hair. 'For now, I say bollocks to Plato. Never mind being virtuous. We live free. We indulge. Forget about the future or the past. Focus on the current moment.' She leaned in close, kissed his neck. 'Focus on—'

'The next five minutes.' He grinned.

She sat up, shocked, then leaned back in again. 'I was thinking at least the next half hour.'

Chapter Five

David Navarro crouched at the side of the chair. He gripped the man's chin with one hand and jerked his head up off his chest. He pushed a gloved thumb onto his eyelid and lifted it, then stared into the eyeball.

Navarro sighed. 'What's his name?'

'Kyle Goddard,' said the unit at the doorway. Cropped blond hair, combat shorts. Ivan Drago spliced with a silverback. He folded his chunky arms across his chest. 'Got his wallet. Driving licence. He's a Brit. Like this pair.'

The two men on the mint-green sofa glanced at each other. One leaned forward, elbows on knees, head in hands; the other sat back, arms at full stretch across the top of the sofa.

Another man, topless, sat perched on the sill of a tall window that looked out to a panoramic beach in the distance, sheltered by towering cliffs. He was short, but toned and fibrous, he wore aviator sunglasses despite being indoors, and his black hair was secured in a small ponytail.

Navarro turned back to the barely conscious man, withdrawing his hand and snapping off his latex gloves. Goddard's chin lolled back onto his chest. 'What the fuck did you do to this guy, Ricardo? He smells of puke.'

The topless man straightened his aviators and tapped the ash from his cigarette out of the window. 'He got sick.'

'Food poisoning or something,' said the man reclining on the sofa. 'Their bog looked like a dirty protest.'

Navarro looked at the unit. 'Hugo?'

'*Retrete*,' the big man translated. 'Toilet.' He stepped forward and cupped his hands, palms up. Navarro dropped in the latex gloves. Hugo pocketed them and went back to his spot.

Their captive groaned, startling Navarro, who stood up and took a few steps back. Navarro was immaculately dressed in light, complimentary colours that accentuated his deep tan: tailored teal polo, salmon pink chinos, grey designer loafers. He was mid-fifties and comfortably the oldest man in the room, but light-footed and trim.

The second sofa man raised his head. He was in bad shape: lank hair, flushed, eyes darting. 'Look. Ricardo. We fucked up. I get it. But what's the plan here?'

The topless man took his time extinguishing his cigarette and flipped it out of the window. He strolled over to the sofa and squatted down. 'No, no. *You* fucked up, Travis.' He pointed to the other man on the sofa. 'Clinton fucked up. I thought we were doing business, not pleasure.'

'Wait, wait, wait.' Navarro walked over to the sofa, put a hand on Ricardo's shoulder. 'Before we work out a plan, explain this to me one more time.'

Ricardo stood, flopped back in the corner of the sofa. 'All was well. We had drinks and tapas. We went back to Travis and Clinton's villa near Arrieta.' He sniffed. 'A little *perico...*'

Clinton took over. 'And then this fucking tool,' he jabbed a finger towards Goddard, 'shouts from his place across the way, "Turn your fucking music down." I mean, there's no need for it, is there?'

'And so you went over there,' said Navarro. 'For what purpose?'

Clinton and Travis looked at each other again.

'To teach him some fucking manners,' said Clinton.

'By screwing his girlfriend?' Hugo stepped out of the doorway.

Travis stood up. 'Listen… It was just—'

Navarro raised a hand, palm down. He lowered it slowly.

Travis sat down again, took a few breaths. 'It just got out of control. His missus was in the back somewhere. Clinton decked him.'

Hugo caught Navarro's eye, translating once more. 'Punched him.'

'And then,' Travis continued, 'she comes out, screaming. I had to give her a slap just to shut her up.' He clawed at his cheeks, let out a strange wailing sound. 'The fucking… *Bitch*. She should have just kept quiet.'

'Clinton beat up this guy,' said Ricardo, 'making him watch Travis with the girl. But he was fucking sick. He couldn't fight back. He said he'd eaten some "bad fish".'

Clinton sniggered.

'What's funny?' said Navarro. He walked over to Clinton, crouched, got in his face. 'I'll tell you. *Nothing*. Nothing is funny.'

Clinton turned away.

'What the fuck is it with you Brits? You get sunshine and cheap beer, and you can't keep your fists to yourselves. And you think it's your duty to fuck the first thing that doesn't tell you to fuck off.'

'Oh, she told him that,' said Clinton. 'She wasn't giving it away. He had to take it. Travis only likes it when he has to take it.'

'Fuck you,' said Travis, under his breath.

'And where is she now?' said Navarro.

'We cleaned up and got them both in the Jeep,' said Ricardo. He lowered his head. 'But she got out.'

'How?' said Navarro.

'I was driving. Goddard was out of it, bleeding all over my front seat. They were arguing in the back. She got the door open when I slowed down, just outside Teguise. There were people nearby. She was shouting, screaming. We had to get out of there.'

'Anyone close enough to get your licence plate?' said Hugo.

Clinton shook his head. 'No way. It was dark. They weren't close enough.'

Hugo stroked the tuft of greying hair jutting from his chin. He stepped closer. 'And did you use anything?'

Travis looked up at him. 'Condom. Kept it.'

'He's not a fucking idiot,' said Clinton. 'This man is a seasoned rapist.'

Travis leapt to his feet, squared up to Clinton, but Ricardo held him back.

Navarro paced. 'Okay. Let's calm down. The plan. First. You know what this is? It's a tragedy. A woman, fucked by this fool. You bring her to me, but she gets away before meeting a real man.'

'We warned her,' said Clinton. 'We said if she said anything, we'd kill him.'

Navarro nodded slowly. 'You're staying with me for a while. Ricardo will look after your villa.'

'How will that work?' said Travis.

'You rented through us, remember?' said Hugo. 'It's not a problem.'

'You got lucky,' said Navarro. 'Ricardo will stay there while Hugo deals with this. If the woman does talk, we don't want police checking and finding it abandoned. She says that three guys did it and took her boyfriend. The police search the nearby villas, but they don't find three guys. So, she looks crazy. They can't prove anything. They assume she's partied too hard with her boyfriend, and he's disappeared. But we can't have the place empty with all your shit lying around.' He glared at Ricardo. 'Keep your head down. No guests. No parties.'

'My boys will go to the couple's villa tonight and clean it up properly,' said Hugo. 'We'll cover the critical details first, watch for police on the major roads coming in. They might not even get an address out of her until we're done.'

'And what about him?' said Travis, nodding to Goddard.

Navarro nodded at Hugo, who walked into the kitchen and came back with a carving knife. He strode over to Goddard and grabbed a fistful of his hair, then pulled back his head and stabbed him three, four, five times in the throat, plunging the blade in to the hilt each time. Blood cascaded down Goddard's chest and splattered down on the stone floor.

Travis sprang to his feet and hurried out to the back porch, retching.

Clinton winced, cracking a strained grin. 'Jesus Christ! Bit harsh.'

Goddard's eyes opened wide. He made a strangled choking sound, collapsed into a brief spasm, then slumped off the chair onto the floor, guided down by Hugo.

A rivulet of blood traced its way towards Navarro's loafers, and he stepped away. 'One problem fixed. Now, if the woman talks and the police run around trying to find her boyfriend, they'll eventually have to give up because Hugo will hide him deep in the El Jable desert.'

Travis staggered back in, keeping his eyes off Goddard.

Hugo walked past him, back out to the kitchen with the dripping knife.

'Look,' said Clinton. 'We appreciate your... hospitality. But we're due back at work in two weeks.'

'That's plenty,' said Navarro. 'Don't worry yourselves. I can fix this. We turn a disaster into an inconvenience.' He walked over to Ricardo and scuffed him around the head. 'As I say. You are lucky. You met up with an idiot, but the idiot has a boss with brains.'

Chapter Six

'All one sees are small succulent plants or thorn bushes in the valley of tranquillity where time seems to have stood still under the pressure of the intense heat.'

Harley pressed her forehead onto the coach window and giggled. 'Is this guy for real?'

Sawyer licked at a lollipop. 'No. It's a recording.'

She sighed. 'I know *that*.' She glared out at the landscape. 'It's all so old and dead. Is anything alive round here?'

'You heard the man. "Even lichens are rare."'

She sat bolt upright. 'Oh! So I should pay attention in case I spot a few *lichens*.' She slumped back. 'Wake me if you see any.'

The coach chugged on, coiling around the narrow dirt road up the side of the mountain. Their fellow passengers shared the usual clichés: the place was *'otherworldly'*, *'like being on another planet'*, *'lunar'*.

They rose through the lava fields, squinting through the grubby windows at the dunes of primeval ash.

The sights could hardly be stranger, but the driver added a dash of synthetic awe by blending a classical soundtrack with the stilted commentary. Jagged string swells, male choral chants, female operatics.

'They've lifted this music from *2001*,' said Sawyer.

'I love that film. My dad watched it a lot when I was little. Didn't understand it then, but that didn't seem to matter.'

'There's a lot going on. The bit where the ape throws up a bone and it cuts to a spaceship?'

She turned. 'Yes!'

'I think he's saying that past, present and future are interconnected.'

Harley snatched Sawyer's lollipop. 'Our past directly informs our future.' She sucked at the tip for a moment, widening her eyes at him.

'At its crest, one notices that the surface of the older section is not completely covered up by the more recent lava.'

The coach rounded the rim of a caldera, and the passengers in window seats peered out on a sheer drop into a fissure of folded magma.

'Not a good time for a landslip,' said a man in the seat behind.

'Fuck's sake,' said his partner.

Harley pinned herself to her seat back. 'My choice tomorrow.'

'The Museum of International and Contemporary Art?'

She shook her head. 'I'll give you a clue. There will be sand. Recent sand. And lovely cool water, as opposed to gritty old ash. And people will bring us cocktails and tasty food.'

Sawyer grinned. 'You love it, really.'

She squeezed his knee. 'I don't hate it.'

'You're indulging me. And you want me to know you're indulging me. So, at least you care that I see you care. I'll take that.'

Harley rolled her eyes. 'I'm just looking forward to a nice beach. But, Mr Sawyer…' She held the lollipop to his mouth, like a microphone. 'Tell me. Why do *you* love it?'

He looked out of the window. The hills were flattening now, the earth tones shifting from grey and brown to red and orange. The coach joined a wider road, leading to a cluster of parked vehicles beside a restaurant and visitor centre.

'It's the mystery,' said Sawyer. 'And the way it's outside of human time. It doesn't pander. It can't be prettified or updated or simplified. It's just here. A product of its past.'

SPECIAL_IMAGE-OEBPS/images/break-rule-screen.svg-REPLACE_ME

The park worker carried the bucket of water to the borehole, emptied in the water and stepped back. A geyser of steam shot up, to laughter and applause from the coach parties gathered around the patch of earth outside the El Diablo restaurant.

A young girl in front of Sawyer called to the man. 'Why does it do that?'

He walked over and crouched to talk to her.

'You can tell he's Spanish,' Harley whispered to Sawyer. 'A British guy would just tell her to Google it.'

The man held the girl's eye. 'You are standing on a volcano.' He patted the rusty ground. 'Not far under here, it is super hot. So, the water turns to gas immediately. It expands and shoots out of the tiny hole.'

'How hot?'

'About five hundred degrees Celsius. When you go for

pizza, that's just a bit hotter than their special ovens. But it's only a few feet under where you're standing.'

The girl gasped and stepped back.

Harley turned away. 'This is so touristy.'

'Not interested in the camel rides, then?'

She looked at her phone. 'I'm interested in the chicken cooked in the heat of the volcano. And, since you're driving, a glass of sangria.'

Sawyer's phone buzzed with a call. He took it out of his pocket and checked the ID.

Harley scowled. 'Who's that?'

'My boss.'

'Does he know where you are?'

Sawyer nodded. 'I don't think he'll be impressed with geothermal heat demonstrations, either.'

'Better see what he wants. I'm going to beat the crowd.' She marched off towards the restaurant entrance. 'Shall I get you chicken, too?'

'Yeah. And a smoothie. Nothing with kale in it.'

She laughed. 'Child.'

Sawyer walked away from the crowd and took the call. 'Sir?'

'Above and beyond, DI Sawyer,' said DCI Colin Hatfield. 'I hope I didn't interrupt your rest and relaxation.'

The park worker launched another geyser.

'I'm watching water dry,' said Sawyer. 'You need a favour.'

'Yes, I do.'

'Can it wait? I'm back next week.'

'Just to clarify, Sawyer. You are still on my shitlist for the lapse at the raid, and for your ill-advised compassion for DI Reeves, who is on my super shitlist.'

'Is there an ultra shitlist?'

'There's an idea. Now, I'm preparing myself to forgive you for Reeves. Your intentions were good.'

Another geyser. 'We know where that leads.'

'Indeed. But the raid balls-up has put a chunky layer of ice around my big old heart.'

'And you're calling with an opportunity to speed up the thaw.'

Hatfield fell into a brief coughing fit. 'If only you could help with my cholesterol as well, Sawyer. Now. Are you sitting comfortably?'

'No. But go on.'

'Leona Fullerton. Twenty-four years of age. She's on holiday with her boyfriend at a villa over there. Near some town called Arrieta. She's currently recovering in Hospital Doctor José Molina Orosa, the general hospital in the capital, Arrecife. No idea who Doctor José Molina Orosa is or was. See, we're old-fashioned in England. We name our hospitals after the location. Makes it easier to direct cabbies.'

Sawyer watched as the park worker gathered up his buckets and the crowd shuffled away. 'Why is she recovering?'

'I'll get to that. Ms Fullerton is the daughter of our esteemed Home Secretary, Nigel Fullerton. And he spoke to the Chief Constable last night. His daughter had called him from the hospital, in tears, saying she was okay but "something bad happened" and her boyfriend is missing. But she was confused and distressed, and he couldn't get much else out of her.'

Sawyer sat at the foot of the stone steps leading up to the restaurant. 'And the Chief Constable called you and asked if you could send someone out to help the local police get to the bottom of it. Because Leona doesn't speak good Spanish and it's upsetting for her to be in a strange hospital.'

'Once again, Sawyer, although it always pains me to say this, you are right.'

'And, without checking if it's okay with me first, you said it just so happens you have a man out here already.'

Hatfield sighed. 'Shitlist, Sawyer.'

'Melting the ice.'

'Exactly. Priorities.'

Sawyer traced a line in the dirt with a finger. 'I'm on holiday, sir.'

'You can carry on being on holiday. All I'm asking is that you take a short pause from being on holiday to go see a young British girl who'll surely be delighted at the sight of those striking green eyes.'

'And is this an order?'

'It's a favour.'

Sawyer looked up to the restaurant doors. Harley waved at him, beckoning him inside. 'What's bad?'

'Sorry?'

'You said she told her dad that "something bad happened".'

'She wouldn't tell him. The Right Honourable Nigel Fullerton MP is at a conference in South Korea. He's due in Lanzarote tomorrow afternoon. The Chief wants me to get in first, though. Good old-fashioned brownie points. They come my way, they get passed to you, and—'

'Shitlist.'

'You're getting it.'

Sawyer looked up again. Harley unfolded her arms and beckoned wildly. He held up a hand and turned away, watching the trails of tourists flowing back onto their coaches. 'What's she recovering from?'

Hatfield paused. 'She was five months pregnant. Miscarried. Her father said he spoke to a doctor who told him she was brought to the hospital by an ambulance that picked her up, alone, at the side of the road just outside a place called—'

'Teguise. I saw it on the local news. So, she turns up from nowhere, miles away from her holiday villa. She's taken to a hospital, miscarries. She calls her dad but locks up when he presses for detail.'

Hatfield blew out a lengthy sigh. 'Rape?'

'Maybe… Missing boyfriend, though. They argued. It got nasty. He dumped her. Maybe he found out the baby wasn't his. That would explain why he lost interest in her welfare.'

He turned. Harley was poised at the top of the restaurant steps, arms folded.

'Just fill in the blanks, Sawyer. Turn your charm on the local plod.'

'My grasp of Spanish doesn't match my level of charm.'

Hatfield gave a wheezy laugh. 'No, but I remember you saying your missus spoke fluent Spanish. See? I may not look like much on the outside, but it's all going in. And it stays in. She's a CSO, yes?'

'She confiscates alcohol from teenagers.'

'Then this'll give her a sniff of the real world.'

Harley started down the stairs.

'I want a transfer.'

'Where?'

'Keating has a new MIT. Up in Buxton.'

Hatfield clicked his tongue. 'There are a few meetings before that happens, Sawyer.'

'Sound him out.'

'We're not haggling. In case you're not clear, I have still got the arse with you. So, you're negotiating from a position of weakness.'

'A favour for a favour. Sir. And you know you can't stay mad at me for long.'

'Hey!' Harley was almost on him now.

'I'm just asking you to smooth the path, Sawyer. Be a… I don't know…'

'Buffer?'

'Yeah. A buffer. Guidance and support. She's a British national, but this is Spanish jurisdiction. Be nice to the Spanish people. Be extra nice to Fullerton. Shake her dad's hand if you meet him. Call him sir. I want to get straight on the phone to the Chief so he can reassure his boss that his top man has got his top man on it.'

'Then you'll consider letting your top man go north.'

'I'll think about it.'

'My mum used to say that when she meant no.'

Hatfield was silent for a moment. 'Consider it considered.'

'Who are you talking to?'

'I need everything,' said Sawyer.

'Everything?'

'On Leona Fullerton. History. Victimology. What brought her to this moment. I know it's not our case, and—'

'And you're on holiday—'

'Yes. But if you want me to help the locals work out what happened to her, and find her boyfriend… She's been brutalised. There might be sexual violence. She's surrounded by strangers. I'll be just another one. I need to know everything to convince her to tell me anything.'

Chapter Seven

Hospital Doctor José Molina Orosa looked more like a well-funded arts centre than a medical facility. The buildings were low-rise and modernist, in pastel green and off-white, marooned on the edge of a scruffy district of car showrooms and wholesalers.

Harley dealt with the parking machine while Sawyer studied the sculpture out front: a gigantic lump of volcanic rock supported on another by a narrow collar of iron, forming an hourglass shape.

She joined him, waving a pre-paid ticket. 'That's the day's food budget blown. You wouldn't go poor investing in hospital car parks.' She peered over her Guccis. 'Haven't we seen enough lava for one day?'

'It's by the same artist who designed the Mirador. César Manrique.' Sawyer turned and headed for the main entrance, followed by Harley. 'That's his work we keep seeing on the roundabouts. He practically curated the place.'

'Mr Sawyer?'

A tall, powerfully built man in a short-sleeved white shirt sprang up from a bench at the edge of reception, trailed by three shorter men in navy blue uniforms and peaked hats.

'Señor Torres?'

The man nodded and shook Sawyer's hand, adding a proprietary pat on his shoulder. 'Comisario Roberto Torres. A pleasure. These are my colleagues from Policía Nacional. I was sent your photograph by my commanding officer, Comisario General Gutierrez, whom I believe has spoken to your superior. I understand you are a Detective Inspector in London? Our ranks are similar. But I suspect you are the busier man.' He grinned, flashing a set of brilliant white teeth.

'And there's also the weather,' said Sawyer.

Torres puffed out his cheeks. 'Oh, it is *too* hot here right now. You know about *calima?*'

Sawyer nodded. 'This is my partner, Sheena Harley.'

Harley smiled and held out her hand.

'Also police?' said Torres, shaking.

'*No soy de un rango tan alto.*' She nodded to Sawyer. '*Pero yo hago el trabajo duro.*'

Torres laughed. '*Español perfecto.*' He turned to Sawyer. 'Apparently, Señorita Harley is not so senior, but she does more difficult work.'

Harley grinned at Sawyer.

'I've been mostly investigating sex parties lately,' said Sawyer. 'She's just jealous.'

Two of the officers exchanged a glance.

Torres studied Sawyer and Harley for a moment. He patted Sawyer's shoulder again. 'You are both most welcome here. My team appreciates your guidance.' He frowned. 'A difficult situation.'

Torres hurried through the hospital lobby, trailed by his red-faced officers, with Sawyer and Harley just about keeping pace. The interior was mint-green and muted blue, and their shoes squeaked on the white resin floor.

They came to a glass double door beneath a yellow-and-black sign marked *UNIDAD DE CUIDADOS INTENSIVOS.*

'Intensive care,' said Harley.

Torres nodded. 'Señorita Fullerton is being... stored in this department as a precaution following her *aborto espontáneo*, which doctors say was late.'

Harley squinted. 'Stored?'

Torres looked to his men. No help. 'Held?'

'*Ella esta siendo cuidada,*' said Harley. 'She is being cared for.'

A young woman in blue scrubs with a white V-neck greeted Torres and swiped a card over a wall panel, opening the glass doors. Torres gestured for Harley to go first, followed by Sawyer and the young doctor, then bolted down the corridor with his men close behind.

'This is Doctor Carmen Garcia-Lopez,' said Torres. 'She is *Jefe de Seccion* here. A senior doctor. She is managing Señorita Fullerton's case.'

Sawyer nodded at Garcia-Lopez. '*¿Habla inglés?*'

She smiled. 'I wouldn't get very far here if I didn't. Not at this time of year.'

'My name is Jake Sawyer. This is my partner, Sheena Harley. We're both UK police.'

'Señor Torres has given me the detail, yes. Señorita Fullerton is... VIP?'

'Yes, I suppose she is in the UK. She's the daughter of a politician. How is she?'

Garcia-Lopez wrinkled her nose. 'Better than I would expect. Anxious. Appetite not good. But she is young and strong. We have completed the… medical procedure with no complication.'

'D&C,' said Harley, wincing. 'It happened to a friend back home.'

'Yes. She is in crisis now, but when that stops she will need emotional support. I know you want to find out what happened to her, but she has been through an upsetting event, and she will need…'

'*Sensibilidad*,' said Harley. 'Sensitivity.'

'*Sí.*'

'She has said very little,' said Torres.

'Did they rent a car?' said Sawyer. 'Fullerton and her boyfriend.'

'Yes,' said Torres. 'We traced it earlier today.'

'Is it still at their villa?'

Torres paused, then glanced at one of his men. '*Su coche alquilado. ¿Todavia esta en su villa?*' The man nodded and replied in Spanish.

Harley leaned in to Sawyer. 'He says there's no sign of the boyfriend.'

'The car is at the villa, yes,' said Torres.

Garcia-Lopez slowed as she approached a side room opposite a uniformed officer sat on a bench.

He spotted Torres, set down his coffee cup and stood to attention. 'Comisario Torres.'

Torres nodded at him and rattled off a strident barrage of Spanish.

Harley turned to Sawyer, holding up her hand as she eavesdropped. 'He's explaining who we are.' She smiled.

'I've been promoted to detective... You're senior detective.'

'If I play my cards right, I might get Hatfield's job by the time we're done.'

Garcia-Lopez opened the door. A young woman in a hospital gown stood by a tinted window overlooking a private balcony. 'Miss Fullerton. Please. You must rest.'

Fullerton sighed and hobbled to the bed against the far wall. Garcia-Lopez helped her back in.

She took a slug of water from her bedside glass and flopped her head back, deep into the pillow, then lay in silence for a moment, chest rising and falling.

She turned her head and surveyed the group. 'When is my father coming?'

'Tomorrow,' said Torres.

Fullerton looked around the group. 'I don't want to talk to anybody until he's here. Any psychiatrists or... social workers or whatever.'

'These people are here to help, Leona,' said Garcia-Lopez.

'Can they get my father here any quicker?'

Garcia-Lopez glanced at Sawyer and Harley. 'No.'

'Well, then I don't want to talk to them.'

'You were told not to say anything, weren't you, Leona?' said Sawyer.

She sat up, searching for the source of the English accent. 'What?'

Sawyer stepped further into the room and hovered by a stack of bedside chairs. 'At first, I thought it could be your boyfriend. But you don't drive. So, someone else must have driven you to where the local men called for help. Your rental car is still at your villa, but your boyfriend isn't. So, I don't think he dropped you off outside Teguise.' He slid out a chair and sat down. 'But this is where I get confused. You've been engaged to Kyle for seven months. He's a gallery curator. A keen scuba diver. You both are. The Canaries seem a little lo-fi for your standing, so I think you're here for the Museo Atlantico. Maybe you're on a recce to see if an underwater museum could work in England. Sorry… Mind wandering. My point is, you're serious. Your joint future was opening up. So, why are you waiting for your father to appear before you tell the local police everything they need to find him? Because someone attacked you both and they still have Kyle, and they've warned you not to say anything or they'll kill him. Maybe you think your father can send it up the chain. Bring in the SAS. You should tell the police here everything that happened, Leona. Your attackers told you they'd hurt Kyle if you talk because they want to slow things down. But he needs you to help police speed this up. The longer you stay silent, the worse it will be for him.'

Fullerton pushed herself upright and took a pair of slender spectacles from her bedside table. She put them on and smoothed out her curly blonde hair. At bedside distance, Sawyer could see her swollen cheeks, forehead bruising. She had a nasty welt across her chin, muted by make-up.

She took a slow drink of water, keeping her hazel eyes on him. 'Who *are* you?'

'I'm a tourist,' said Sawyer. 'Back home, I'm a Detective Inspector with the Met. My name is Jake Sawyer. This is my partner, Sheena Harley.'

Fullerton nodded. 'Is she a copper, too?'

'Sort of,' said Harley. 'We've been asked to help, Leona. But you need to help us.'

'Your father's not here yet,' said Sawyer. 'But he's signed off our involvement. So, until he arrives, you might as well treat us as the next best thing.'

Harley looked around the room. 'You seem to know a lot about me, Mr Sawyer.'

Sawyer edged the chair closer. 'I'm sorry this happened to you. And I'm so very sorry for your loss. But you're safe now. Detective Torres and his team are capable officers. You should give them what they need, for Kyle's sake.'

Fullerton took off her glasses and lowered her head.

'Leona, you told your father something bad happened. What was that?'

Fullerton stayed silent.

They listened to the distant hustle in the lobby, a tannoy announcement, the swoosh and ping of a tall stack of monitor machines wedged into a portable frame at Fullerton's bedside.

Tears tapped onto her sheets. She kept her head down, tremoring and sniffing.

Eventually, her eyes raised to Sawyer. 'They hurt me.'

'Who did, Leona?'

She reached for a tissue, blew her nose. 'Two of them.'

'Names?' said Torres, stepping forward. 'Did they use names? What did they look like?'

Sawyer held up a hand. 'Were they under the influence of alcohol or drugs? Did they hurt Kyle?'

Fullerton let out a jagged, elongated groan. She wiped her eyes with another tissue. 'Not alcohol. But it was like… Two of them were on something. Red faces. Grinding their teeth… There was a third guy. He wore dark glasses, even at night. He seemed sober. More together.' She jerked her head around, aiming her raging eyes at all the faces in turn. 'Look, just... Fuck off! Okay? *Everyone.*' She grabbed a double fistful of bedsheet and pulled it up over her head. 'I don't want this. I can't *do this.* I'm sorry, I'm sorry, I'm sorry.'

Sawyer and Harley followed Torres back out to the lobby. His pace was slower this time; a borderline saunter. His men kept to a group on the far side of the corridor; one spoke on his phone, while another wrote in a small pad.

Sawyer dropped back. 'Can you hear what he's saying?' he asked Harley.

She held up a hand, listening. 'Not really. He's speaking so fast, I can't... Something about a Nissan? Red. And... *geared up?*'

'Forensics. They must be sweeping the couple's car. Probably at their villa. *Perdón.* Comisario Torres?'

Torres reached the door to the lobby. He stopped and turned, smoothing down his greying goatee. 'Señor Sawyer.' He smiled, a little forced.

'Do you mind if we join you at the couple's villa? If that's where you're going next?'

Torres's smile broadened. 'Yes. I do mind. But I'm happy to make an exception. Just this once.'

Chapter Eight

Fullerton and her boyfriend had rented a modest villa on an open patch of land in Arrieta, a fishing village with a few basic tourist concessions: tapas bar, serving-hatch takeaway, grocery store stocked with exotic bread and baffling confectionery. The stark white facades of the traditional houses were accented by blue and green doors and shutters, and the cobblestone lanes spilled through the streets and squares, down to the seafront.

Sawyer clambered up onto a raised section of undeveloped land a few yards along from the couple's villa where Torres's team had gathered. A small group out front in white overalls, face masks and shoe covers swarmed around a red Nissan Qashqai.

Harley joined him, panting in the heat. She took a glug from a bottle of water, looked over at the CSIs. 'The PPE looks posher.'

'Probably its first time out of the box.'

She whispered. 'They're wearing *goggles*, Jake.'

Sawyer surveyed the space at the back of the village. A

group of local children chased a football around a scaled-down pitch beside a toddlers' play area, their shouts clinging to the feeble breeze. A lone seagull wheeled and shrieked.

'Imagine living here,' said Harley.

'I was about to say that.'

'No, you weren't. You were about to say something profound about the indifferent ocean or something.'

He squinted at her, shielding his eyes from the sun. 'You're setting a high bar for a man who's had no lunch.'

She shoved him. 'Yes! We need to eat. Let's see what they have at that tapas place.'

He took a drink from her bottle. 'Good luck with that. For an hour or so, at least.'

Harley reeled away. 'Fucking siestas.'

'They have those at the Amalfi Coast, too.' He headed down to the street. 'Sort of.'

She followed. 'It smells like Hull. Fishy.'

'That'll be the fish.'

'I had a boyfriend from Hull. He was such a mansplainer. Mostly bloody rugby league.'

Torres ducked out of the villa's main door and walked across the small courtyard. He spotted Sawyer and came over.

'Anything interesting?' said Sawyer.

Torres shook his head and lit a cigarette. 'It is early to say. I think we will maybe find out more when the father arrives tomorrow. Things might open up.'

'You'd be surprised. It's usually the opposite. With a rape.'

Torres puffed out smoke. 'How did you find out? Did you speak to the doctor?'

'No,' said Sawyer. 'It's the shame. The way she

couldn't tell her father the whole story on the phone. The way she covered herself up at the hospital. Self-blame. If this was a plain assault or a robbery, we would have a lot more by now. Misplaced though it is, she probably has triple the guilt. For herself, her boyfriend, her unborn baby.'

Sawyer caught movement from a villa on a corresponding patch of land opposite. A hulk of a man in loose white shorts and a florid short-sleeved shirt emerged and strolled over.

Torres tapped ash onto the ground. 'Mr Sawyer. Your help is welcome, of course. But I must consider… *prioridades.*'

'Priorities,' said Harley.

'Is it clean inside?' said Sawyer.

'*¿Perdón?*'

'The villa.'

'It is. Smells fresh. Very tidy. Not what we usually find with Brits abroad.' He grimaced in disapproval. 'Perhaps a woman's touch.'

'*¡Hola!*'

They turned. The man from the villa reached them. From a distance, he had looked large. Up close, he was immense; scaled up in every direction. There would be cardiovascular benefits to taking a walk around him.

'Can I help?' said Torres.

'I was going to ask the same question.' The man smiled, but the look clashed with his overhanging brow, rendering his upper and lower face like a mismatched e-fit. 'I live across the way. We don't get too much excitement here.' He gestured to the couple's villa. 'I saw the police cars and the people out front. I hope everything is okay.'

'Thank you,' said Torres. 'But we have things under control.'

'I see you are police.'

'Roberto Torres. Comisario. These are colleagues.'

The man shook Torres's hand. 'Esteban Guerra.' He leaned in close to Torres and spoke in a low voice; he was gruff and spoke lightly accented English, hard to place. 'As a matter of fact, I almost called you last night.' He held on to Torres's hand, still shaking.

Torres glanced at Sawyer. 'Why is that?'

'There was a lot of noise coming from that house. The couple there. I've seen them come and go. They were arguing. It was so loud I had to turn my TV up.'

Torres eased his hand free. 'What do you do, Mr Guerra?'

'Oh, I'm a letting agent. I own several properties around the island.'

Sawyer nodded to the villa where Guerra had come from. 'Do you live there?'

'I do when it gets this hot.' Guerra took out a white handkerchief and patted his cheeks and the grey fluff at the point of his chin. 'I prefer the sea air when *calima* comes.'

'Did you hear what the couple were arguing about?' said Harley.

Guerra watched the CSIs. 'Something about money. It was getting quite heated.'

'Is it your property?' said Sawyer.

'No, no. If it was, then I would be making sure the tenants respect their neighbours more.' He nodded to the CSIs. 'I hope nothing serious has happened. Are the couple okay?'

Torres took a puff on his cigarette and eyed Guerra. 'The investigation is… in progress.'

Guerra nodded and pulled on another ill-fitting smile. 'Of course. I wish you well. I'll keep an eye out for anything suspicious.' His eyes wandered over the three of them for a moment, then he turned to go.

'You're a bad liar, Mr Guerra,' said Sawyer.

'I'm sorry?'

'I don't think you heard the couple arguing.'

Guerra held Sawyer's eye. 'Ah. You mean… Could I have mistaken them for another couple?'

Sawyer shook his head. 'The couple renting the villa aren't short of money. People with money don't argue about it.'

Guerra laughed. 'Well, maybe I misheard that part…'

'I imagine you're right about the lack of excitement round here. So, I'll give you the benefit of the doubt and assume you couldn't resist coming over and spinning a story to add a bit of spice. Don't worry about keeping an eye out, though. We've got it covered.'

Guerra's features cycled through a spectrum of emotions: confusion, concern, irritation, anger, and then a slow blush of amusement.

He slapped Sawyer on the shoulder. 'You're a funny man, Mr—'

'Robbins,' said Sawyer, after a pause.

Guerra gave a strange little wave and plodded away, head held high. They watched him complete an unhurried journey back to his villa, and he disappeared inside without looking back.

'Why did you tell him your name was Robbins?' said Harley.

'I don't think he gave us his real name. Why should I?'

Torres stamped out his cigarette. 'Strange that he would come over like that.'

'Exactly,' said Sawyer. 'You often see people involved in a crime insinuate themselves into an investigation.'

Harley scoffed. 'He might just be nosy. A bit of a busybody.'

'Felt like he was fishing,' said Torres. 'Asking if everyone is okay.'

Sawyer nodded. 'He also gave us something, in the hope of getting something in return. The stuff about arguing.'

Harley gave an exaggerated stroke of her chin. 'I'd say he's a creepy, or lonely, guy with too much time on his hands. Trust me, there are a lot of them around.'

Sawyer turned to Torres. 'Comisario, did your men find any phones in the couple's villa?'

Torres hesitated. 'No.'

'So, you have phone data?'

He sighed. 'We do.'

'And Leona Fullerton didn't have her phone when the emergency services picked her up?'

'No. She doesn't remember what happened to it. We have both devices tracked from here to a final mast ping near Famara Beach.'

'How long is that journey?'

Harley took a few steps away and looked down an alley that led down to the harbour.

'Around half an hour. It is difficult to get to Famara from here because of the mountains. From the phone data, it looks like they cut across through Teguise and doubled back. I would do the same.'

Sawyer thought for a moment. 'We're not looking for clever people here, Mr Torres. If they abducted this couple for a specific reason, then they would surely know the phones could be tracked.'

Harley turned to them. 'Or… They're cleverer than we think, and they took the phones to leave a false trail. They've dumped the boyfriend's phone at this Famara place and then gone somewhere completely different, to put us off the scent.'

Torres and Sawyer looked at each other.

'Have you taken swabs from Fullerton?' said Sawyer.

Torres paced for a moment. 'Detective Sawyer,' said Torres. 'Señorita Fullerton is safe. Her father will be with us tomorrow. I will of course make it known to Comisario General Gutierrez that your help has been welcome. Please. Enjoy the rest of your holiday. This is now a matter for Policía Nacional.'

Chapter Nine

Sawyer raised his taco to his mouth with both hands and paused as he caught Harley's quizzical look.

'A posh Filet-o-Fish,' she said.

He took a bite and swept his gaze around the terrace diners, burnished in gold by the retreating sun.

'You said I wasn't allowed to have the paella,' said Sawyer, mopping his mouth with a napkin.

Harley took a forkful of her own food. 'That's hardly the exotic option.'

'So, I'm abusing your system.'

She sipped her rosé. 'Jake. You have the palate of a… teenager.'

'Thank you for not going any lower.' He ate, nodded at her dish. 'Your rice is black.'

'Yes. *Arroz negro*. It's a traditional Spanish dish. They add squid ink for look and flavour.'

'I use soy sauce for that, and I'm fine with white rice. I won't be grain-shamed.'

She hit him with an epic eyeroll. He smiled and stared

out over the bay. The undulating dunes lurked in the twilight at the edge of the terrace decking. Throbbing hip-hop rose from a gathering at the base of one of the volcanic cliffs that shielded the cove. Despite its expanse, and the hour, Famara Beach was smothered by amblers and meanderers, trotters and trudgers; loungers, floppers, Instagrammers. Dogs lolloped along the shoreline, swerving the surf. Boarders clung to the waning ripples.

Harley looked back at the Dunas de Famara dining room: an upcycled bistro, in the round, with a lively bar at the heart of the action. Tangerine chairs, sandstone curtains, handwoven candy-stripe cushions. The place spanned the demographics—contemporary splendour, boho soul—with a soundtrack of woozy downtempo: swaying beats, piano sprinkles.

'This is a nice place,' said Harley. 'Good choice. Not cheap, though. I assume you're buying?'

'Can we not be gauche?' He took another bite.

'Do you know how much CSOs make?'

He nodded.

She flipped her hair, let down for the night, over her shoulders and looked down at the white stones arranged along the decking border, fringed with spindles of cacti. She touched a finger to a spine.

'Ow! They're sharper than I thought.'

Sawyer watched her, finishing his mouthful. 'You're suspicious.'

'What?'

'You're thinking this isn't my kind of place.' He took a swig of Diet Coke.

'Why does that make me suspicious?'

He shrugged. 'If it's not my kind of place, then why did I bring you here?'

Harley smiled and swirled her wine around the glass. 'This is how it works, Jake.'

'How what works?'

'Relationships. You know… Compromise. Like you said at the volcanos, you're indulging me. This might not be your thing, but you've brought me here because you know I'd like it. There's a podcaster I listen to. Dan Savage.'

'Isn't he the sex therapist?'

'Amongst other things. He says partners need to be three things. Good, giving and game. Shorthand, *GGG*.'

Sawyer nodded. 'And this is my GGG moment?'

She beamed, kissed him. 'Yes, it is. Thank you.'

He read a sign above a building further along the beach: Lanzasurf Yoga & Massage.

INHALE PEACE

EXHALE LOVE

'I heard Esther Perel quote Jack Morin,' said Sawyer. 'He said that attraction plus obstacle equals excitement.'

'Uhuh. Is that why we go for bad boys?'

'Not necessarily. Just that we don't want what we can easily have.'

Harley nodded, pondering. 'Do you think some people prefer the wanting to the having?'

'I think some worry about what comes after the having. So they settle for the wanting.'

She squinted, processing. 'Sometimes, easy is okay, Jake. Just enjoy the moment.'

He knocked back his Coke. 'Will you do something for me?'

'Depends on what it is.'

'Ask a young waiter the locations of the most expensive properties around here. Where would he live if he could afford it?'

Harley squinted at him. 'Why?'

'GGG.'

She didn't respond, browsed the menu. 'Would you care for dessert? There's crumble.'

'What kind?'

She leaned in with an evil grin. 'Pineapple and chilli.'

Sawyer wrinkled his nose. 'Here's what should be in crumble…'

'Apple?' said Harley. 'Nothing else, right?'

He thought for a moment. 'I suppose I could choke down a hint of cinnamon for a special occasion.'

'Why do you want to know about expensive places to live? Are we moving here after Stamford Hill?'

He snapped off a shard of taco, crunched it like a crisp. 'Torres said that Fullerton and her boyfriend's missing phones last pinged near here. I like your idea about the abductors using the phones to put us off the trail—'

Harley cut in. 'But Fullerton said she thought two of the three men were on something.'

'Yes. I don't think they were clever in the first place. Certainly not on drugs.'

'Coke?'

'Probably. She said they were flushed. Teeth grinding.'

Harley flopped back in her seat. 'And what about our friend in Arrieta?'

'The big guy?' He shook his head. 'What do you think?'

She smiled. 'Oh. Is this training college now?'

'No. Just… what do you think? I want to know your perspective before mine influences it.'

Harley tapped her fork on the table. 'The clothes.'

'Go on.'

'Didn't look right. Loud shirt. Shorts. He seemed uncomfortable in them.'

Sawyer nodded. 'Almost like a disguise. Not his usual style.'

'Trying too hard to look friendly and laid-back.'

'Yes. And Torres said the couple's villa had been recently cleaned. It smelt clean. That's more than just tidying and trying not to leave anything obviously incriminating.'

Harley took a mouthful of her black rice with crab. 'Go on, then. What's in the envelope?'

'Envelope?'

'As in Cluedo. Colonel Mustard. Lead piping. Dining room.'

Sawyer looked out to sea. The horizon had almost smothered the sun. Tendrils of cloud wafted in, concluding the performance. 'I think Leona Fullerton was raped by two of the three men, while the other one dealt with her boyfriend. The attackers panicked, probably tried to tidy up the evidence, but then thought it would be better to take the couple away from the house and get it professionally cleaned. They could then let them go, and they could tell the police whatever they liked, but there would be no evidence.'

'So, where were they taken?'

'Whatever the destination, Leona ruined the plan by

escaping at Teguise. They stopped somewhere around here, threw their phones into the sea…'

Harley looked up to the cliffs. 'From up there?'

'If it were my investigation, I'd have forensics up near the edges. We might get a cigarette end. DNA.'

Harley put a hand on his. 'Yes. But it's not your investigation. And you still haven't told me why I'm asking where the best houses are.'

Sawyer's phone buzzed.

'Fullerton said that only two out of the three men were on something. That makes me think the third guy supplied it. So, there's a good chance he's a dealer, or at least connected to a dealer. And drug dealers live in the best houses. One sec.'

He got up and walked away from the dining tables out to the edge of the decking and took the call.

Harley twirled her bracelets as she waited. It was dark now, and dress-shirted waiters emerged to light overhead lamps.

Sawyer came back, sat down.

'Who was it?' said Harley.

'My friend Nigel.'

She frowned. 'Nigel?'

'The Home Secretary. His daughter wants to talk to me first thing tomorrow.'

Chapter Ten

David Navarro wheeled his turquoise Arne Jacobsen swivel chair away from his desk and pinched open the vertical blinds on the floor-to-ceiling window.

Clinton and Travis had colonised the covered back terrace beside the raised infinity pool. The curved rattan loungers had been yanked out into direct sunlight and surrounded by magazines, snack packets, beer bottles.

Clinton swam up and down, length after length. Travis lay on a lounger with a book.

'We'll need to shock the pool the second they're gone,' said Navarro. He shuddered. 'It'll be a fucking soup. Dead skin cells. Atomised shit.'

Hugo Krueger reclined in the corner of the low, liquorice-black sofa that spanned the facing wall. 'All those chips and pies and beer.'

'Don't.' Navarro rolled back to his desk, sipped from a glass of orange juice. 'Order some new loungers, too.'

Krueger frowned. 'The Serpentes aren't cheap.'

Navarro tipped his head back and stared up at the ceiling fan. 'I don't care. Some things you can't scrub off.'

'The couple's villa is clean.'

'I appreciate it. But we're not *cleaning*, remember. We are erasing events. Re-ordering the past to make the present more favourable.'

Krueger gave a slow nod. 'Like the boyfriend. He's with El Jable now.'

Navarro looked at him, grinned. '*Calima* will bury him deeper.'

The ceiling fan thrashed overhead. Navarro tipped his head back and savoured the relief. '*Mierda*. This heat.'

'Maybe it's finally time to get air con,' said Krueger.

'That's when we start catching each other's viruses. Or get everyone's skin particles blown down our throats. Or the heat we can't feel warms up our drinks, breeding bacteria.'

A loud shout from Clinton outside made Navarro startle. Then a splash.

'I want them gone.'

Krueger angled his head. 'Gone?'

'Away. Back to Britain. I want this business back on track.'

Krueger got to his feet, walked to the window and peered out at Travis and Clinton. 'It'll be done in a few days. The police will find nothing at the villa. But the girl might ID them, so we keep their heads down. Ricardo is there now. He knows to lie low. Any sign of police, he calls me.'

'It would be safer to—'

'We need him. For now.'

Krueger watched as Clinton took a running jump into the pool.

Navarro winced at the splash and shout. 'Can't we just chain them up in the basement like naughty pets?'

Krueger turned, shook his head. 'They're clients. Hard to believe now, but they're key to the connection. You could see it as a good thing. Gives us more leverage, for our trouble.' He walked back to the sofa, took a sip from a glass of beer on a side table. 'We keep sight of them here. The police trail goes cold. The search for the boyfriend turns up nothing. We send them back separately.' He set the beer back down. 'Events erased.'

'Coaster,' said Navarro.

Krueger took a small circular beermat from a stack on Navarro's desk and slipped it under the glass. 'We keep track of the investigation. Whatever the police say they look like, we make sure they look different. If we have to get them out on forged passports, the Brits can pay.'

'And how are they taking it all?'

Krueger took a long drink, set the glass back down carefully in the centre of the coaster. 'Ricardo is smoothing it over as a glitch.'

Navarro nudged his wireless mouse, waking the screen of his enormous iMac. 'You saw the police by their villa?'

'Yes. I tried to plant it as a domestic. They didn't buy it. But they don't know much.'

'Who was the detective?'

'Torres.'

Navarro sighed and loaded up a word game. 'Who else?'

'How do you mean?'

'You say "they".'

Krueger flopped back in the sofa. 'There was a man and woman. More Brits. The man said his name was Robbins, but he was lying.'

'How do you know?'

Krueger pinched his thumb and forefinger together. 'Just took a little too long to come up with the name. He was good, though. Smarter than Torres, that's for sure.'

Navarro shoved his mouse around its mat, highlighting and linking blocks of letters packed into a tower shape. 'British police?'

'Maybe. I'll get Ricardo to speak to Mateo. Find out who he really is.' He snatched up the beer, drained the glass. 'Nothing to worry about.'

Chapter Eleven

'I read about you.'

Leona Fullerton leaned over the balcony and drew on her cigarette.

Sawyer glanced in through the tinted French windows. Torres and two of his men hovered near the door while Harley sat on the bedside chair. Garcia-Lopez perched on the end of the bed, looking out at them, arms folded.

'Your doctor isn't happy about the smoking.'

'Takes the edge off. First one I've had since I found out I was pregnant. Not an issue now.' Her voice cracked and she turned away.

It was early morning, and scandalously hot. A sandy haze fuzzed out the distant mountains. Sawyer approached the railing, giving Fullerton plenty of room. The hospital car park below was already busy with circling rentals, hunting for spaces. Both ticket machines were surrounded.

'Queuing,' said Sawyer. 'One of the few areas where we Brits still lead the world.'

Fullerton lifted her sunglasses and looked down. 'Are they even queues?'

'It's the class system that makes us good at queuing. We instinctively re-order ourselves by status. Who gets the privilege? Who's next? Who's last in line? It's comforting.'

She coughed out a smoky laugh. 'My father would like you. I share his political ambitions. I think he's secretly disappointed that I'm not the typical posh-girl rebel. Sabotaging hunts, protesting cutbacks.'

'That's one kind of politics.'

She shrugged. 'Change always comes from inside the system.'

'What did you read?'

'About you?' She sat down on a bench by the window. 'Good God. About what happened to you when you were a child. I'm so sorry, Mr Sawyer.'

He nodded. 'Did you read it or ask your father to research me?'

'Well. That. Of course. But my father didn't do it. He had some civil servant look you up.'

'He called late yesterday. He didn't go through the Chief Constable. Or my DCI. They won't enjoy that.'

Fullerton turned to him sharply. 'I told him not to. Keep it direct.' She gestured to the room behind, lowered her voice. 'I don't know these people, Mr Sawyer. I'm scared for Kyle. You know what it's like. Continental types. No urgency. They take two hours to finish their lunch before attending child abduction scenes. Look at the Madeleine McCann case.'

'Are they "continental types"? We're almost in Africa.'

She took a long drag, puffed smoke to the side. 'Spanish jurisdiction, Spanish law, Spanish corruption. They've been riddled with scandal for years. Top to bottom. Judicial to *ayuntamientos*. Town halls. Check the Corruption Perceptions Index. Spain is barely above Eastern Europe, where corruption is endemic. Practically cultural.'

Sawyer took a drink of watery hospital coffee. 'So, you did your homework on me.'

'You did it on me. And there's not much else to do in here. I mean, how on earth did you survive with your...' She took another drag. 'I'm sorry. This is the last thing you want to talk about.'

'I'm a Stoic.' He sat on a cheap chair, scraped it closer. 'I choose not to suffer.'

She gazed at him. 'Are you in therapy?'

'Let's talk about Kyle, Leona. I'm fine, but his life is in danger. What happened to you both? If you can give me the whole picture, I might be able to help. And this isn't you show me yours and I'll show you mine.'

Fullerton got up and walked to the railing again. 'We'd had a nice evening at a seafood restaurant in Orzola. But Kyle wasn't feeling well so we went back to the villa.'

'I've seen it. Did you have different food?'

She paused, nodded. 'He had some seafood platter thing. I can't stand seafood. So, we got back to the villa... There was a place nearby. It sounded like they were having a party. Really loud music. Kyle was trying to rest on the sofa at the front of the house, near a cloakroom. I got him some water and went out to the back of the house, to take a bath. When I came to check on him, maybe fifteen minutes later, they were there. Beating him up.'

'Who were?'

'Three men.'

'Can you remember anything they said?'

She thought for a moment. 'Two of them were British. Southern accents. The other one with dark glasses didn't speak.' Her voice wavered, and she pushed her fingers through her hair. 'Two of them held me. Kyle tried to get back into the bathroom to be sick. The third guy let him, and then dragged him back out. One of the British guys said something like, "We should be telling *him* to keep the noise down."' Fullerton closed her eyes and gripped the balcony. 'The one with long greasy hair pushed me onto the sofa. The guy in dark glasses held Kyle back. He tried to help but he was just too sick. The one with greasy hair… I saw him put on a condom. It was quick but violent. He kept slapping my face. Sometimes punching. Like he had to do it to stay interested. I tried to scream, to tell him I was pregnant. The other one held my head and kept his hand over my mouth.'

'Did he not… attack you?'

She opened her eyes, nodded. 'He tried. Dragged his friend off. Couldn't manage it. He took it out on Kyle.' She extinguished her cigarette and held the balcony with both hands. 'Good God, Mr Sawyer. They beat him badly. Kyle is such…' She choked back the tears. 'Such a beautiful soul. The bastard who tried to rape me kept hitting him and hitting him. In the face. There was blood.'

The hammer. Rising and falling.

His mother's shock and outrage.

Her hand reaching up, trying to grab the hammer.

His dog, dying, but still barking and barking.

Sun flaring through the blood in his eyes.

Sawyer shifted the chair back, into the shade. 'What then?'

'Then, the one who didn't speak brought over a car and they got us both into it.'

'He didn't say anything at all?'

She pondered. 'Maybe a little bit. But he was whispering to the one who couldn't get it up. Don't remember anything he said. He took our phones and, I think, told the other two to tidy things up while they kept us locked in the car. Poor Kyle was just flat out.'

'And where did they take you? Do you remember anything they said about where they were going?'

Fullerton shook her head. 'I think the car was some kind of Jeep. You had to climb up to get in. The guy with dark glasses was driving, with Kyle in the passenger seat. They had to slow down, near a town.'

'Teguise,' said Sawyer.

'I started to shout and scream and one of them tried to shut the window. I grabbed at the handle and got the door open. There was a garage. Petrol station. I kept shouting and screaming. I expected them to try and get me back in, but they just drove away. Then I remember some local men checking on me. An ambulance came. Police…' She startled at a memory. 'There was this house. Lots of weird statues and dolls in the garden. Like some kind of art display.'

'Do you remember anything the men said when you managed to get out? They might have panicked, forgot themselves, referred to each other by name.'

She caught her breath. 'Yes. One of them said, "Leave her! This isn't one of your fucking books. It's real!"'

'Books?'

'I'm certain. It's stuck with me, for some reason. I

might have just been delirious and… The weird statues and sculptures. I remember the night sky, and how bright the stars were…'

A tremor rolled through Fullerton, and she squatted down, holding the balcony. Sawyer rushed over, got his arm round her.

Garcia-Lopez slid open the French window.

'It's okay.' Fullerton held her hand up. 'Please.'

'Mr Sawyer,' said Garcia-Lopez. 'She needs rest.'

Fullerton glared at her. 'I said I'm okay.'

The doctor retreated.

Sawyer helped her up and guided her back to the bench. He brought over the coffee.

'Best I can do, sorry. I couldn't get the gin past your doctor.'

Fullerton sipped at the coffee and put a hand to her stomach. 'You know… He only started to kick after the attack. I'd felt him move before. But only kicks since. Before… Before he left us.' She spoke through sobs now, recovering then speaking. 'I feel so fucking *empty*, Mr Sawyer. Like a part of me has been ripped out.' She looked at him, eyes wild. 'Those *bastards* murdered my child. Even if you find them, you can't change that. What am I going to do? How will I ever be the same again?'

Sawyer crouched beside her, then sat on the floor. 'You won't be. Now, you focus on survival. On thriving yourself, despite this. You choose not to suffer. Don't let it poison you. Define you. You've been changed by something you couldn't control. Now, you have to reinvent yourself. Work on the change you can control. Grieve for your loss. That might not be easy, Leona. It's different for everyone. But you do have to try. Because grief is love.'

Sawyer caught movement in the room: Torres and his men barging past Garcia-Lopez, heading for the window. He took Fullerton's hand. 'I'll do what I can to help the police find Kyle. But you have a long life ahead of you. You're strong. You'll discover what you need to do to survive. Before you can do that, though, you need justice. Believe me. I know how that feels.'

Torres slid open the window and stepped onto the balcony. 'Señorita Fullerton. Your father has landed.'

Torres led the way down the corridor, ahead of Sawyer and Harley. He upped the pace as they reached the lobby door and swiped everyone through.

'Please excuse me, Detective Sawyer. I must prepare for Señorita Fullerton's father. He is due within the hour. Can I ask, did you learn anything new out on the balcony?'

'Lots of things,' said Sawyer. 'First, though, I have a few questions for you.'

Torres smiled, flashing those teeth. 'Quick questions.'

'Is there some sort of art exhibition outside Teguise? Leona said she thought she saw a house with statues and sculptures in the garden.'

'Ah. She means the Casa Museo Mara Mao. That's the home of a local artist, known as Don Pillimpo. He takes discarded items and remakes them into art. Dolls, teddy bears, televisions. It is something of a local tourist attraction. How does this matter?'

Harley showed Sawyer a website on her phone. *The House With The Statues in Teguise*. The photos showed a white-walled garden crammed with random statues and pop-culture artefacts.

Sawyer studied it. 'I thought she might have been hallucinating. But it looks like she's a reliable witness.'

'What else did she tell you?' said Torres.

Sawyer hesitated. He glanced at Harley. 'She was sexually assaulted, Mr Torres. By two British men. A third man, possibly Spanish, was an accomplice. He assaulted Mr Goddard, Leona's boyfriend. The men tidied up after themselves and drove the couple through Teguise, where Leona escaped.'

'I appreciate the help,' said Torres. 'We will take steps—'

'Did your forensic team find evidence of bleach at the couple's villa?'

Torres sighed. 'I believe so.'

'In areas that wouldn't normally be bleached?'

'The floor in the sitting room. A few other surfaces.'

'And do you have any more on the DNA? I'm sure you found traces of latex in the vaginal swabs. Leona said one of her attackers wore a condom, while the other couldn't get it up. You should be looking for places where he might have purchased the condoms. Start local and fan out. And do you have skin scrapings from Leona's fingernails? If these men are British, then we should be working together with DNA records in the UK. What about fingerprint—'

Torres reached down and took Sawyer's hand, lifting it from his side. He shook it and slapped his shoulder with the other hand. 'Detective. I don't wish to be rude. But I feel your work on the case has finished. We have everything we need to track down these men and find Señorita Fullerton's boyfriend.' He shifted closer. 'She is soon to be back with her father. My men are professionals, and they will continue to work hard to solve this case.' He lowered his voice. 'Let me educate you. Lanzarote is an autonomous community. We are under Spanish sovereignty, but we have self-governing powers. We are certainly not a British colony.'

Sawyer kept his eyes on the squeaky white floor. 'I wish you the best, Señor Torres. But I suspect Leona's boyfriend is already outside both our jurisdictions.'

Chapter Twelve

Harley ducked in through the beaded door curtain and staggered into the sitting room, dripping pool water. She took a bottle of Evian from the fridge and laid out her towel in the centre of the room, beneath the ceiling fan.

'Fuck! Just heard someone say it's thirty-three degrees.'

She flopped out on the towel, starfish style, chest rising and falling.

Sawyer sat reading in a shady corner, on a lumpy green armchair with stubby wooden legs he'd levelled with folded tourist pamphlets. He was topless, in cherry-red trunks, feet folded underneath him.

'I was just reading about it. A *calima* last year pushed it up to forty.'

Harley whistled, sat up for a drink, lay back down again. She looked over at Sawyer. 'You have good legs.'

He smiled, kept his eye on *The Outsider*. 'Have I?'

'Yeah. Muscular but not too beefy. What's that thing you do?'

'Thing?'

'Karate thing.'

He glanced up, then back to the book. 'It's called Jeet Kune Do. Like mixed martial arts. A bit of everything. I also trained in Wing Chun-style Kung Fu. You've heard of Bruce Lee?'

'The movie star, yes.'

'He conceived JKD as a philosophy. It's all about finding the most efficient path. Simplicity. A style with no style. Most martial arts have strict rituals and pre-set moves. He threw all that away, saying it wasn't realistic.'

'But he made lots of movies, right? Using unrealistic moves.'

Sawyer shrugged. 'Real fights don't look good on camera. He said you should follow principles but also use whatever's available. Improvise. Be creative. And, yeah. The films are entertainment.'

She laughed. 'I've seen one. The bad guys all just wait around while he takes them down, one by one.'

'Exactly. But he knew opponents in real life aren't predictable.'

Harley lay back, starfished again, legs spread wide. She looked over. 'Actually, your knees are a bit knobbly.'

'Is this negging?'

She laughed. 'No. Just trying to get you to look. You have a hot blonde girlfriend in a halter neck Versace bikini, prostate on the floor beneath you, and you're more interested in a dead French existentialist.'

Sawyer laid the book flat. 'Prostrate.'

She smiled. 'I knew that would get your attention.'

Sawyer tapped at his phone and started some music. Woozy vocal behind a trudging lo-fi beat.

'Who's this?' said Harley.

'They're called Washed Out. Well, he is. His real name is Ernest.'

Harley sniggered. 'No wonder he changed it.'

They listened in silence for a while, lightly roasting.

'Got a craving,' said Harley.

'What?'

'Kettle Chips. Cheddar and red onion.'

'That's a trip to the big grocery by the baker in San Bartolomé.'

She sighed, flopped back. 'I have to say, it's growing on me.'

'The island or here?'

'Both.' She swept a hand through the air. 'I love this place. It's decorated like they're about to do a *Condé Nast Traveller* shoot. Moroccan and Indonesian influence. Earth tones. Lots of terracotta.'

'I suppose the word is *authentic*.'

She sat up. 'I just like the way it feels natural. In tune with the location. Surrounded by vineyards, orchards, gardens, instead of just some ghastly resort that panders to guests who only come for the weather.'

'There are plenty of those on the south of the island.'

'You're a country boy, though. You understand. It's the peace. The hush. Even the birds seem to sing quietly.'

Sawyer got up and walked through to the bedroom. 'The birds don't sing. They screech in pain.'

'What?'

'Sorry. Quote from a film. Herzog.'

Harley followed him, watched him change into shorts and T-shirt. 'You said it yourself. You liked it because it's a… product of the past. The eruption. And it doesn't change.'

'Yeah. It exists outside our timescale. It doesn't care

about our human business. It'll be the same a long time after we've gone.' He slipped on a pair of khaki Vans. 'It'll be here a long time after Leona recovers. All the horror she's been through equates to just the tiniest blip in time.' He caught her eye. 'You're going to say this is depressing.'

'No. I can see why that would be a comfort to someone who'd been through something awful. Something human-made. Where are you going?'

He jangled the car key. 'Kettle Chips. You can stay for a siesta. Since you're going native. Pull out some early Spandau Ballet.'

She nodded, suddenly pensive. 'There's a little albino patch on the back of your head. Just at the crown. Did you know?'

'Yes. It's not something I think about much, though. I don't get to see it very often.'

Harley stared into space. 'You know what I think, Jake?'

He froze. 'Go on.'

'I think Kyle Goddard is dead.'

Sawyer gathered some cash. 'I agree. Why do you think that, though?'

She pondered. 'Why take the risk? If you're vicious enough to assault the couple like that, you're probably vicious enough to finish them off. Leona is lucky to be alive.'

'Exactly. Maybe the attackers knew who they were, knew who she was. But, as far as we know, there hasn't been any ransom demand. I don't even think it's a home invasion. More like a chance encounter that spiralled. As with most crime, it's a continuum of bad decisions. Someone is trying to whitewash it. Abducting the couple was the start of that. They're going to a lot of trouble.'

'Which means there's more at stake than just a couple of tourists who crossed their path.'

Sawyer headed for the door; she followed. He opened it then stopped and turned. 'You didn't ask why I don't think it's a home invasion.'

Harley sighed. 'And I was doing so well.'

'Leona told me one of the men said something about how her boyfriend was making grim noises while being sick and said that *they* should be the ones complaining about the noise.' He paused, but Harley just shrugged. 'She also said she found the men beating up Kyle when she got out of the bath. I think he complained about the noise they were making, and they took exception.'

'So, they were nearby?'

He nodded. 'And Torres said someone had used bleach on their villa. On the floor. I can hear a voice in my head. A forensic pathologist I know.' Sawyer imitated a light Glaswegian accent. '"There are more red flags than a bullfighting convention."' He switched to his normal voice. 'Nobody uses bleach on a floor. Certainly not midway through their stay. And nobody cleans up with bleach unless they absolutely, positively don't want forensics using luminol to show up bloodstains.'

'Blood shows up in weird places, though, doesn't it?'

'Yep. There will be a splash somewhere they haven't considered. Unless they were thorough and used luminol as part of the clean-up. You never get it all, though… It's the speed of the clean-up that's the biggest alert. It's sophisticated, organised. They've done it before. This isn't just two coked-up tourists sticking a mop round. Like I said, there's a lot more going on here. Leona Fullerton was right not to trust the locals.'

Chapter Thirteen

Sawyer drove through the charred badlands surrounding Casa Tomarén and headed northeast, past low-rise whitewashed houses flanked by drought-resistant shrubs and succulents, past walled-off vineyards planted into hollows of patchwork soil.

The blacks and browns segued to greens and yellows as he merged with the coastal road and turned into Arrieta.

He left the car in a quiet spot near a demolished building above the harbour, and walked up the road past the couple's villa, still cordoned off, with two of Torres's blue-shirted officers out front, smoking and leaning on a patrol car.

The heat blared down, and he tugged on a white baseball cap and slunk into the shade, diverting to a vast tract of developed land that housed several detached villas.

Sawyer lingered by a telegraph pole and acted out a dummy phone call as he observed Esteban Guerra's two-storey villa across the way from Leona and Kyle's.

No cars outside. No obvious movement inside.

He waited for two tourist couples to pass by on their way through to the harbour, then approached the front door.

Three short raps. No answer.

He repeated. Still nothing.

Sawyer took out a pair of Harley's kirby grip hairpins and opened one out until the ends sat at a ninety-degree angle, then inserted it into the keyhole and bent it to one side, shaping it into a kink. He twisted the other part of the pin back on itself, fashioning a handle.

He paused to take a quick look around, then slid the other straight hairpin into the keyhole, using the kinked pin as a wrench and the straight pin as a pick. He took a breath and pulled and twisted the hairpins, subtly shifting their position, feeling for the cylinders that held the lock in place, opening them one by one.

As he released the final cylinder, the lock clicked. He took out the picks, turned the handle and stepped inside, relocking the door behind him.

The place smelt sour: turned food, decaying fat, unflushed toilet. He covered his mouth and nose at a kick of sulphur.

Sawyer walked down the hall into a palatial open-plan kitchen with six tall grey-and-black stools scattered around a central dining island. A host of flies mobbed an overflowing bin in the far corner.

Full ashtrays on the dining island. San Miguel bottles.

He walked through the kitchen into a sitting room.

More flies, hovering and swooping above a stack of takeaway cartons on a circular glass coffee table.

More beer bottles. Soiled napkins. Another full ashtray.

Safety matches. Guillotine cigar cutter.

He had a look in a pouch of Pueblo tobacco. Half full.

Sawyer crossed the sitting room and walked down a short hall into a huge en suite bedroom. Floor-to-ceiling windows opened onto a private sea-facing balcony around the side of the house.

Wooden furniture. Rustic armoire: open and empty. Lavish wrought-iron headboard on a bed large enough to sleep four.

A car slowed on the road at the front side of the house.

Sawyer paused, listening as the engine idled and cut out.

He opened the cupboard and drawer of a bedside table. Empty.

The other table's drawer was full of heavy-duty Italian pornography. The cupboard held a stack of paperbacks.

Stephen King: well thumbed. James Ellroy: first few pages broken in, but the rest unread. James Patterson, Lee Child.

The car engine hadn't restarted.

He took out a couple of books, flicked through the pages. A folded sheet of paper fell out of a copy of *Along Came A Spider*.

Voices outside. Male and female. Mostly male.

Sawyer unfolded the paper. It was a printout of an email. An Airbnb booking confirmation to traviswheeler87@gmail.com. Two weeks. Two guests.

Male shouts from the back door. A key in the lock.

The door crashed open. Chatter in Spanish.

A woman, keening. Coquettish chiding.

Two male voices rose and fell in mock protest.

Sawyer pocketed the paper and replaced the books. He checked the balcony window. Locked.

He lifted the lid on a bright yellow ottoman at the foot of the bed. English newspapers. A small key.

Loud laughter in the kitchen.

And now, footsteps, heading through the sitting room to the bedroom.

Sawyer ducked into the bathroom, lit with a small skylight.

He pushed open the heavy wooden door and pressed himself behind it.

Wait for them to leave. Get the key. Out.

He would have to take stronger action if the visitor discovered him. There was no other escape route.

A man entered the bedroom. He snorted, rattling phlegm at the back of his throat.

Sawyer looked around the edge of the door. His reflection was just visible in the mirrored tiles above the double sink.

He inched closer to the wall behind the door, fully out of sight.

Shouts from the kitchen.

The bedroom door clicked shut, muffling the kitchen noises. Had the man left the room or just closed the door behind him?

Sound of a handgun cocking.

'*Salir.*'

Sawyer sighed. '*Inglés.*'

'Come out. Now.'

Sawyer walked around the door, hands raised.

A man stood at the top of the bed, gun aimed at Sawyer. He was topless, in loose white shorts, matching sliders and aviator sunglasses. Short, toned, black hair scraped into a ponytail. He held the gun high and horizontal.

'I saw you in the mirror, *culero*. Out here. Now.'

Sawyer strode out into the bedroom.

'Slow.'

He jabbed the gun forward and Sawyer stopped, a few feet from the man, keeping his hands high.

Sawyer winced.

The man scowled at him. 'What?'

'Side grip,' said Sawyer. 'Seriously? *New Jack City* was a long time ago.'

He smiled. 'You want I hold the other way? No problem. I'll still take off half your smartass fucking head. Who the fuck are you? You know Krueger? What are you doing in there?'

'Just checking the walls.'

'The *walls?* What are you, man?'

'I'm a contractor.'

The man studied Sawyer with concern. 'I know the owner of this house and he doesn't have any jobs here right now.'

'I got lost. I get confused in the heat.'

The man nodded, smiling. 'You know. Here we are. All alone. I might be the last thing you ever see. You should be shitting your pants.'

Sawyer shifted his footing so he was almost side-on to the man, left foot forward. 'I don't really do that.'

'What?'

'Fear. And anyway, you should be the scared one.'

'Why?'

'No offence. But you don't look like the brains of the operation. If I were you, I'd be worried how my boss will react when I tell him I had the jump on an intruder and didn't shoot him. Also, I'm not a doctor, but I know a melanoma when I see one.'

The man frowned. 'What do you mean?'

'Skin cancer. Malignant melanomas tend to be asymmetrical. Not the same on both sides. And the border is usually ragged. Both those things are true of the lesion on your right shoulder. You should get yourself to a dermatologist.'

The man held Sawyer's eye.

He turned his head and raised his aviators, glancing down at his shoulder.

Sawyer pushed off and lunged forward with a Wing Chun *biu jee* strike, jabbing the man in the eyes with rigid fingers, sending the sunglasses flying. His head jerked back, and he staggered, but kept hold of the gun. Close in now, Sawyer pivoted and hit him in the chin with an upward elbow strike, driving the full force of his body into the blow, snapping the man's head back.

He dropped the gun, toppled back into the bedside table and lay slumped in the corner, out cold.

Sawyer checked his pocket and pulled out a wallet. He found the driving licence and took a photo on his phone before slipping the licence and wallet back into the man's pocket.

He took the key from the ottoman and unlocked the window, sliding it open quietly.

Sawyer was about to step outside, but he stopped, looked over his shoulder at the man and smiled.

He walked back to the bedside table.

Chapter Fourteen

Back at Casa Tomarén, Sawyer found Harley flat out on the bed beneath the mosquito net. He slid his laptop out of his carry-on case and quietly retreated to the sitting room with a cold Diet Coke.

He set the laptop up on the carved wooden coffee table and spread the printed Airbnb booking confirmation out by its side. After a few minutes of searching and cross-referencing, he found the second villa listed on Airbnb, booked out for the rest of the month, and used a filtered search to find multiple listings from the same host. The properties were mostly luxury villas dotted around the eastern side of the island, with a few more centrally located.

Sawyer shifted the laptop out onto the terrace and made a call. A male voice answered, too loud. London accent.

'This is Reeves.'

He turned the volume down. 'This is Sawyer.'

A pause at the other end. 'Blimey, Sawyer. Are you cashing in already?'

'How's work?'

A Zippo clicked, as DI Max Reeves lit a cigarette. 'You know when your missus wants you to know she's over something, but she's still pissed off with you? That's Hatfield. My niece calls it "pass-agg".'

'I'm looking into something out here for him. He should cheer up soon.'

He puffed out smoke. 'And is this an official call?'

'Not yet.'

'And will Hatfield be happier or sadder if he finds out I helped you?'

'Definitely happier. But don't tell him yet. If this doesn't work out, I'll keep your name off the books. If it goes well, then your contribution will have been essential.'

Reeves wheezed a laugh. 'Success has many fathers. Go on, then.'

'I'm going to send you a list of properties in Lanzarote, and I'm hoping you can tell me about the international reputation of their listed owner, Navarro Holdings.'

'Fair enough. Anything else?'

Jake? Harley, from the bedroom.

Reeves spluttered. 'Sounds like you left the toilet seat up.'

'Also, I have a Gmail address. Traviswheeler87@gmail.com. And a plus-44 number. Both linked to a booking for one of the properties. I have the date the booking started, so you should find Mr Wheeler on the passenger manifest for a flight from the UK to Lanzarote on that date. Plenty of detail on his priors, if you'd be so kind.'

'Well, that's one for the intern.'

'One more thing. I was rudely accosted by a local earlier. Ricardo Ruiz. I'll send you a picture of his driving licence. See what you can dig up. Same with two other names. Esteban Guerra. Ruiz also used a surname. Krueger. See if they come up when you're rooting around. Guerra is probably a fake, but it might help join the dots.'

Reeves paused. 'Roger all that. So, this puts us nice and square, yeah? For you saving my marriage and keeping me clear of a misconduct hearing.'

'It's a start,' said Sawyer, and hung up.

Chapter Fifteen

David Navarro tapped at his keyboard, peering down at each key as he typed, slow and methodical.

He glanced up. 'How long?'

Hugo Krueger looked at his phone. 'Just arriving.'

'Go easy.'

Krueger paced. 'He's a big boy. How are the guests?'

'They don't get up until midday.'

'Fucking Brits.' Krueger tugged at his beard. 'How did these bastards ever run the world?'

'Naval power,' said Navarro. 'Also, industrial revolution. Trade routes. But the money isn't there anymore. Technology has globalised everything.'

Krueger pinched the bridge of his nose. 'We had to cancel the party here tonight. *Noche en Blanco*. Still a big night for us, though. We could do without this.'

The door opened and closed downstairs.

Navarro shouted. 'In the office!' He stopped typing and sat back at his desk, holding Krueger's gaze for a moment.

Krueger pulled the door wider as Ricardo entered. He barred the way, then reached over and lifted Ricardo's aviators.

Navarro rose to his feet and lapsed into a fit of laughter.

'*Puto coño,*' said Ricardo, as he snatched back his sunglasses and crashed down on the liquorice sofa.

'Is that my employee,' said Navarro, 'or a fucking *panda?*'

Both Ricardo's eyes sported deep purple bruising around the sockets and across the bridge of his nose. He wore a thick strip of plaster over a wound at the base of his chin.

Navarro strolled over and looked down at him, hands in pockets. 'Now, are you ready for our meeting? Are you sure you don't need to masturbate first?'

Ricardo sighed, replaced the aviators with care. 'He left the magazine out.'

'Why?'

'To humiliate him,' said Krueger.

Navarro peered down at Ricardo, head tilted. 'Taking your gun off you wasn't humiliating enough?'

'He didn't take my fucking gun. He hit me with a sucker punch. He didn't fight fair.'

Even Krueger cracked a smile at that. 'Well, Ricardo. You learned something, at least. Fairness is for losers.'

Navarro took a bottle of water from a mini fridge near his desk and set it down in front of Ricardo. 'Carlo said he found you in the bedroom. Alone. The girls were with him.' He sat down beside Ricardo, wrapped an arm around his neck. 'Not you. We need to talk about our reputation.'

'*Jake Sawyer,*' said Ricardo. He looked up at Krueger.

'It's the guy you told me to look for. He's not *Robbins*. I spoke to Mateo. One of Torres's men told him he's helping because of the couple.'

'Because they're Brits?' said Krueger.

Ricardo took a drink, nodding. 'And her father's some kind of politician.'

Navarro stood up and ambled back to his desk. 'What is he? MI5?'

'Detective,' said Ricardo.

Krueger walked over and crouched down in front of Ricardo. 'And did you tell him anything?'

'Of course I fucking didn't. I should have shot him in the face when I had the chance.'

'No, you shouldn't,' said Krueger. 'You did the right thing. You must have heard that knowledge is power?' He stood upright. 'Things that we know… We know who he is and why he's here. He doesn't know that we know that. We know he's suspicious of me. Why else would he be snooping round the Brits' villa where he last saw me? We know he's armed.'

'How?' said Navarro.

Krueger nodded to Ricardo. 'Why would he let him keep his gun if he didn't have one himself?'

Navarro looked between the two. 'This is supposed to make me feel better? Did he find anything?'

'Nothing to find,' said Krueger. He nodded to Ricardo. 'Apart from his junk food crap and porno.'

Ricardo sighed and lowered his gaze.

'Clear out of there,' said Navarro. 'If you want a base to indulge yourself, I'll find you somewhere down near Playa Blanca. But don't bring anything back to the annexe here.'

Ricardo nodded, slow and ponderous. 'Another thing we know. This guy is fucking *loco*.'

Krueger shook his head. 'No, no. He's smart. He read me like a cheap novel.'

Ricardo sat forward. 'You weren't there, Hugo. I had a gun in his face, and it was like he was taking a walk on the beach. Most people, you point a gun at them, they'll tell you they wear their grandmother's underwear. This guy was smiling. Making fun. This wasn't front, either. *Cojones*.' He looked up at Navarro. 'It was like he wasn't even scared. Like he wasn't right in the head.'

Krueger scoffed. 'You just didn't find his level.' He walked to the window, turned and perched on the sill. 'I spent two years in Pollsmoor, Cape Town. It's not a prison. It's a holding pen for hell. Seven thousand souls jammed into space for four thousand. They round up the worst of the worst, grind them down, goad them into killing each other. It's cheaper than feeding them or putting them on trial. There's no rehabilitation at Pollsmoor. Most inmates are tied to gangs, and so there's no leverage to get them to behave. The whole system is designed to dehumanise the inmates. Shrink them down so they're either desperate to die or hungry to kill. Anyway, there was a guy there. Kosie. He was a Suidlander.' He shook his head. 'Hardcore neo-Nazis preparing for a race war. He was their top boy. Untouchable. The high priest of the alphas.' Krueger ran his fingernails across his beard, back and forth. 'His fucking eyes, man... He had this look. It was like... He could steal your soul. So, he got sick one time, just before a cell spin. Normally, his status meant they left his place alone. But this time he wasn't there so they took advantage.' Krueger walked over to Navarro's desk and placed his hands on the edge, leaning forward. 'They found a fucking giraffe. A cuddly toy. So, the screws turned detective. They checked old family photos and saw a young girl in the background of one, holding the giraffe. They worked out it was Kosie's daughter. Nobody knew he'd had one. And she had died at five years old, from anaphylaxis. From then on, the screws had him in their pocket. They rationed his access to the giraffe, threatened to make it public.'

'This is hardly an unfamiliar idea, Hugo,' said Navarro. 'The Achilles heel.'

Krueger wagged a finger. 'I know, but this was deeper than that. It wasn't just a weakness. It was like it was part of him. In his bones. A fault line he could never fix. Everyone has one, including this guy, Sawyer. You just have to find it.'

Chapter Sixteen

Sawyer slipped out of bed early and faced the bathroom mirror in his underwear. He took a few breaths and lowered into Wing Chun horse stance. He tucked his fists in tight to his chest and fired off fifty straight punches, keeping each action strong but controlled, rolling his fists over each other, hitting the same point in the air at chest height.

This was morning meditation: structured, efficient, repetitive. Drilling the centreline principle; embedding its simplicity.

Sawyer showered and took his le Carré novel out to the breakfast room, settling on the side terrace with milky coffee and chewy granola.

He eyed the book as he munched on a slice of white toast with honey. His efforts with *Tinker, Tailor, Soldier, Spy* held an internalised comedy. As sure as a toilet break seems to activate a long-awaited parcel delivery, any attempt to read more than two or three pages would yield a chronic distraction from which there was no return.

He left it unread, gazing at the cover's brooding blue-on-black type as he sipped his coffee and inhaled the loamy aroma of the ashen soil at the edge of the pathway that ran through the grounds.

His phone buzzed with a text message. He checked the ID on the notification window: *Dad*.

Jake. The Klein parole hearing is set for late summer. You should know he might get out this time. But not if I can help it. Call me. Much love.

Sawyer spooned more honey onto his toast. This was his father's way. Insider information dressed up as speculation.

But not if I can help it.

Meaning, don't trouble yourself.

Meaning, stay out of it.

He had to move soon, or risk telegraphing his intentions once Klein's release was confirmed.

He scooped in a few mouthfuls of granola and made a call. It connected immediately.

'Working on Saturday, sir?'

'Don't you start,' said Hatfield. 'I've had this from my better half. She thinks I'm choosing overtime ahead of a trip to Streatham Vale Homebase.'

'She's right.'

Hatfield coughed out a strained laugh. 'I'll let that go, Sawyer. Because I'm happy to report that you've successfully moved off the shitlist and you are now in the waiting area for my good books.'

'Why the waiting area?'

'Well. In the blue corner…'

'Is that good?'

Hatfield sighed. 'What?'

'The blue corner.'

'Yes. There's a red corner, alright? That's bad. I'm getting to that.'

'Can I go red first?'

'No, you fucking can't. As I was saying. Blue corner. The Chief is happy with your hands-across-the-Atlantic efforts. I hear the Home Sec contacted you personally. Did he send you a basket of muffins?'

Sawyer lay back in his creaky wicker seat and stared up at the unblemished blue sky. 'I just did what you asked, sir. Smoothed the path. Many thanks for your help with victimology, by the way.'

Hatfield spluttered. 'I didn't help you. I was going for a shit and collared a DS who was trying to hide Facebook from his screen when he saw me approaching. But you made your mark. The Chief says their top man sends his thanks. El Presidenté or something.'

'Comisario General Gutierrez.'

'That's the one. Mission a-fucking-complished, Sawyer. He says they're confident they can finish the job.'

'They've hardly started it.'

Hatfield laughed, without mirth. 'There you go. That brings us nicely to the red corner. Hear this, Detective Inspector. The man who's ready and willing to help with your transfer request is officially telling you that it's time to get back to being on holiday and leave this business to Lanzarote's finest.'

Sawyer slurped his coffee. 'This is becoming a theme.'

'What is?'

'People telling me to move on. To leave things alone.'

Hatfield left him hanging for a while. 'Sometimes, that's good advice. You're not Dirty Harry, Sawyer. If I haven't blown enough smoke up your arse, here's a bit more…' He made an extended puffing sound down the phone. 'You really didn't hear this, but I've spoken to Keating. He's in. You and Reeves need separating, anyway. You're like the naughty boys at the back of the class. Answer me this, though.'

'Go on.'

'Why go back?'

Sawyer poked at his cereal. 'A new challenge.'

'This is me, Sawyer. Not the HR manager.'

He thought for a moment. 'It's grim up north. Maybe it'll be less grim with an effervescent soul like me in it.'

'A northern soul,' said Hatfield.

Chapter Seventeen

Harley slapped a hand onto Sawyer's leg. 'Did you know,' she looked up from her phone, 'Lanzarote is a biosphere reserve?'

He gripped the steering wheel tighter as he weaved along the rugged dirt road. 'UNESCO clearly didn't make it down here.' The sandy *calima* haze was moving in now; it almost engulfed the peaks of the Los Ajaches mountains, squatting further inland.

'Playa de Papagayo,' announced Harley. 'I chose this beach for two reasons. One, it's beautiful…'

'You've been before?'

She slumped her shoulders, mock teenage. 'Instagram. Two, it's hard to get to. So, it won't be too crowded.'

He laughed. 'The heat is evil. It's a beach. It'll be crowded.'

'Do you know what a biosphere reserve actually is?'

'Something to do with sustainability?'

Harley gazed at him, beaming. 'Gold star.' She

checked her phone. 'They're "learning places for sustainable development".'

'That sounds oxymoronic.'

She narrowed her eyes at him. The front wheel on her side clunked in and out of a crater. 'Actually, make that three reasons. The name. Papagayo.'

'Sounds like an exotic fruit you only find in Waitrose.'

'It's Spanish for parrot. Opinion on the music?'

He listened for a moment. 'George Michael?'

'Wham! This is called "Blue".' She prodded him. 'It's the B-side of "Club Tropicana".'

He smiled. 'A deep cut.'

'Yes. Fan favourite. Post-disco pop. And it's brilliant. Like the comedown after the high of the A-side.'

They listened, lurching and dipping through a brutal sequence of pits and furrows.

'Can't you see I'm falling apart?' said Sawyer. 'He's been here, too.'

She shoved him, singing along.

Sawyer caught a hint of ozone in the air as the road crested and, finally, levelled out. Harley cheered and raised her hands as the swimming-pool blue cove water twinkled into view.

SPECIAL_IMAGE-OEBPS/images/break-rule-screen.svg-REPLACE_ME

They sat at the tip of the Be Papagayo restaurant terrace, under a thatched parasol, and watched a steady flow of tourists shuffling down a narrow path to the beach below.

'Fancy a catamaran cruise?' said Harley, working through sardines with cherry tomato salad.

'I thought you'd never ask.'

Sawyer finished his scrambled eggs and ham, and

leaned over the low whitewashed wall to get a better view of the coastline: a line of circular coves nibbled into the rock. Craggy lava cliffs shielded the fans of golden sand, stilling the transparent waters.

'Busy,' said Harley. 'But so beautiful.'

'You could say the same about Alton Towers. And they have rollercoasters.'

Harley took a sip of wine and rested her hands on his; pink nails, bracelets clinking. 'I need those green eyes, Mr Sawyer.'

He obliged, holding her gaze as she leaned in.

'So, what now?' she said.

'Walk on the beach? Lemon sorbet?'

'How are we feeling about that life of virtue?'

He smiled. 'Hard to sustain.'

She sat back, returned to her wine. 'You know that annoying habit you have?'

'Only one?'

'You read minds. You tell people what they're about to say.'

A salty breeze ruffled Sawyer's hair. 'I read people. It's my job.'

'Well, I'm just a humble Community Support Officer, but here's my attempt.' She managed a weak smile. 'You're not planning to make my mother happy, are you, Jake? I get the sense you have other priorities.'

He sighed. 'It's the picture, isn't it? The one you saw me looking at in the Mirador.'

'Of course. Wouldn't you be curious, if the roles were reversed?'

'What do you want me to say? You know the story.'

'Only the version everyone else knows.'

Sawyer picked up a menu, turned it round in his

fingers. A phrase was written in curlicued blue script across a patch of white space at the back.
SONRIE. RESPIRA. VE DESPACIO.

'Smile,' said Harley. 'Breathe. Go slow.'

He looked out to sea, fixated on a chugging passenger boat labelled *WATERBUS*.

'His name is Marcus Klein. He's been in prison for almost thirty years. He tried to get parole a few times. He first tried after fifteen years, but he must have pissed someone off in the process because they adjusted his minimum to twenty. He appealed, right up to the European Court.'

'Human rights?'

Sawyer nodded. 'But they didn't buy it. They kept him in Wakefield Max for the first five. He didn't so much as cough in the direction of an officer, so they shifted him to Cat B. He's been in Cat C for the last ten. Not a sniff of trouble. Looks like he's in line for an oral hearing very soon. Given his record, if they don't release him or at least drop him to Cat D on licence, he'll appeal again, and he'll win this time. The Home Office knows that. So, they'll save some money and let him walk.'

'And why do you care?'

'They say he murdered my mother.'

She groaned, squeezed his hand.

A diner at a nearby table adjusted her wide-brimmed sun hat and her long black hair whipped around her shoulders.

Sawyer felt the nausea rise. He closed his eyes, willing it away. But there was no escape.

His mother's face, pulverised. Rearranged.

His dog, thrashing in the grass. Then twitching, then still. Mortally wounded by the same hammer.

His big brother in a crumpled heap, showered in blood. His blood, and their mother's.

Sawyer's phone rang: a violent vibration on the table that startled him.

'And you don't think he did it?' said Harley.

He took a breath, checked the ID.

Reeves.

'I know he didn't. I want to help him clear his name. Get his life restarted.'

'How?'

He stood up. 'Working on that. I need to take this.'

'So, if Klein didn't murder your mother, who did?'

'Working on that, too.'

SPECIAL_IMAGE-OEBPS/images/break-rule-screen.svg-REPLACE_ME

Sawyer took his Diet Coke and wandered round the back side of the branded shop connected to the restaurant building.

He accepted the call.

'Whenever you're ready, Sawyer,' said Reeves. 'Busy at the local flea market?'

'I was about to get you something nice.'

'Well, I'd take a local wine, if it's not too much trouble.'

Sawyer turned, putting his back to the beach, looking up at the filling car park. 'Actually, I had my eye on some erotic Canarian pottery.'

'Not my bag. I dare say Travis Wheeler would be keen, though. He's a bad boy, Sawyer. Exposure. GBH. Sexually assaulted a teenager on a Tube train a couple of years ago. He was collared after a vile gang rape at a private club in Wandsworth. Didn't stick, but only because the accuser backed out. Minor drugs offences. He was on a plane that arrived in Lanzarote five days ago.'

'Anyone with him?'

'He reserved his seat online, and added Mr Clinton Hines, in the seat next to him. Tickets are returns. Two weeks. The Airbnb booking also includes Hines, so I assume they're besties. Hines is another charming character. Did five years for GBH on an ex-girlfriend. Broke her arm, but his brief convinced the jury it was unintentional. Bit of light forgery. Importing watches. He's also picked up a few drugs offences.' He paused, closed a door, lowered his voice. 'Now, here's the good bit. Both Hines and Wheeler are associates of an OCG that the NCA broke up last year. The big boss, Keith Kent, was a long-standing dealer and he pumped his profits into turning a garage into a fucking amphetamine lab.'

'Sounds like a TV show.'

'I know. Cancelled after one series, though. The NCA busted the lab after a tip-off.'

'*My First Breaking Bad.*'

Reeves snorted. 'Very good. So, Hines and Wheeler were named as part of the investigation, but they weren't there during the bust. Fucking spawned it. Kent and his cronies all went down, but...' He paused for effect.

Sawyer watched as a pair of waiters came out of a kitchen and stood together, smoking.

Reeves huffed. 'Come on, Sawyer. The sun must be making you dopey.'

'Kent has links with continental dealers.'

'That's my boy.'

'And one of them has something to do with this Esteban guy I met.'

'You're close. I couldn't find anything on Esteban Guerra. As you say, probably made up. But the owner of the property company you gave me... We're touching the top tier now. David Navarro. I ran him past Interpol NCB in Manchester. They're investigating possible links with South American drug cartels. The other guy, Ruiz. He's Colombian. My Interpol contact says that because the Canary Islands are just off the coast of Africa, they're a key transit point for drug smuggling from South America via West Africa. The OCGs exploit the ports and maritime routes and shift drugs up into mainland Europe where they're easier to distribute. And here's my favourite bit. Before his garage lab got taken down, Keith Kent was tracked in Lanzarote, as a guest of—'

'David Navarro.'

'Bingo! I mean, fuck me twice, Sawyer. You're supposed to be on holiday, but it looks to me like you've stumbled on some kind of business deal between Navarro and Kent's operation in the UK, with the two British jokers in their Navarro-owned Airbnb as go-betweens.'

Sawyer turned to the shop window. Recyclable water bottles. Mini cacti. Diffusers, wax burners. 'Do you have a business address for Navarro Holdings?'

'I can do you two. Looks like a place in Arrecife, the capital, and another somewhere called... Vista la Graciosa. I'll send them over.'

'Thanks for this, Max.'

'Never a chore.'

'Did you get anything on the name Ruiz let slip? Krueger?'

'Ah, I almost forgot. That's got to be a geezer called Hugo Krueger. Interpol did a search of Navarro's file for me, and Navarro unwisely used his real name when he bailed Krueger from an arrest a few years back in Morocco. He's also a partner in Navarro Holdings. South African. A shit-ton of porridge for violence, drugs. Father was a police officer in Johannesburg. Corruption allegation when Krueger Jr got off a murder charge.' Reeves opened the door again. Background office noise filtered through. 'Listen, I'm gonna leave this rabbit hole in your capable hands now, Sawyer. If I were you, I'd pass on the intel to the Spanish police and get straight back on that plane to Blighty.'

'You're not me.'

Reeves laughed. 'No, I fucking am not. And knowing you, I'm glad.'

Chapter Eighteen

They drove back to Casa Tomarén through a baked yellow smog. Windows closed, air-con roaring. Locals wore face masks, while tourists covered their mouths with cloth. Despite the heat, a boisterous wind swirled across the lava fields, whipping ash through the clotted air.

Harley propped her bare feet up on the dash and swept a hand across her thigh. 'There's dust everywhere.'

'Sand,' said Sawyer. 'From the Sahara.'

She sighed. 'Yes. I'm hoping it won't bring in weird insects.'

He glanced across. 'I read that happens. Locusts, dragonflies, ladybirds.'

'I'll take a plague of ladybirds.' She squinted at the display. 'Wow. It's thirty-eight.'

'Dry heat, though.'

She laughed. 'My mother says that. Still not sure what it means.' She scrolled through her phone. 'They say to stay inside. Drink water, keep windows and doors closed.' She squeezed his thigh. 'Sounds like you'll be stuck in an air-conditioned villa with a rampant blonde for the evening.'

Sawyer kept his eyes ahead. 'Did you talk to the waiter?'

'What? Oh, at Famara? Yes. He said the area near to the beach is built-up but there are a few luxury properties set back where *pijo* live.'

'*Pijo?*'

'Posh. Rich.' She turned to him and leaned into the seat, knees pulled up. 'Do you think they've found the boyfriend yet?'

'No. And they won't. Like you said, the people who attacked the couple don't want to leave a loose end. They won't risk finishing the job by attacking Leona because it's safer to let it all fade away. Into the past. There might even be collusion.'

Harley gasped. 'With the authorities here?'

He nodded. 'If there's high-level interest in keeping the case unsolved, it won't be solved.'

'What do you mean, high level?'

'Dirty police. Or clean police with an insider. Criminal gangs with overseas paymasters.' He flicked his eyes over. 'I think I'm ready for another go at the Cluedo envelope.'

She twisted round to face the front, tied up her hair. 'We go home in two days. Weather permitting.'

'You said you wanted romance. Adventure is romantic.'

Harley stared him out.

'What?'

'It's not your fight, Jake. You've done what you can.'

'*No.*' It came out too loud; he softened his tone. 'I haven't. Would Kyle Goddard's family agree that I've done all I can? We could fly home, leave Leona Fullerton to her recovery, and the men who attacked her would be free to do the same to another woman. We could abandon Kyle's family to the agony of limbo. Or we could open the envelope. We could do more.'

Harley turned away again. 'Real policing.'

They closed the shutters and holed up in the sitting room, sprawled in their swimwear on the cool tiles.

Harley dunked her glass in a champagne bucket full of iced orange juice and lemonade and took a long drink. 'So, the villa in Arrieta is booked out for the next month. But Hines and Wheeler were due to return to the UK in a couple of weeks.'

Sawyer smiled and slid a slice of pizza from the carton onto his plate. 'So?'

Harley frowned. 'They're not there now.'

'Looks more like it's being used as some kind of party house. And they wouldn't be stupid enough to hang around there, in case Leona's account leads to police checks near the couple's villa.'

'So, where are they?'

'Exactly. Reeves gave me two addresses for the company that owns the villa.' He opened his laptop and navigated to the browser, with tabs he'd saved earlier. 'One is for a unit in a trading park just outside the capital. The other is a detached house near Famara Beach. I think David Navarro has people run Navarro Holdings for him from the place in Arrecife, and he lives in Famara Beach.'

Harley shuffled closer and took some pizza. 'So, he wanted to get a connection to deal drugs in the UK…'

'Not deal,' said Sawyer. 'Looks to me like he's a distributor. He might even be a lieutenant who reports to a kingpin at source, probably in South America. The dealers are street level. The guy who confronted me, Ruiz, will be a link in that direction—'

'And this Krueger is Navarro's deputy?'

Sawyer shook his head. 'It feels like they're closer than that, given Navarro bailed him one time. I'd say he's more of an enforcer, looking at his record.' He took a drink. 'So, go on. Open the envelope.'

Harley sat back and chewed her pizza, thinking. 'He wanted to get a connection to the UK. This guy linked with Hines and Wheeler...'

'Kent.'

She nodded. 'He sends them over here to set everything up... They stay at the villa across the road in Arrieta. Kyle and Leona come home to their villa, which is in earshot. Kyle is sick, and Wheeler and Hines are playing loud music...'

'I'd say Ruiz was the third man Leona mentioned.'

'Kyle shouts over to tell them to keep it down. They're hotheads, coked up, and they come over to confront the couple...'

'Leona is in the bath. She comes out to find Kyle being beaten. They assault her.'

Harley winced. 'Sounds like Wheeler would have started that, given his history.'

Sawyer nodded. 'Yes. Then, they panic. Ruiz drives everyone to Navarro's, planning to clean up and remove the evidence. But then Leona escapes. Navarro probably decided to kill Kyle and have the villa deep-cleaned before Torres's team got there. That explains why Krueger, AKA Guerra, was so interested the day we were in Arrieta.'

Harley pointed at him. 'So, Navarro stashes Hines and Wheeler away somewhere, while Krueger and Ruiz hold the fort at the other villa.' She gasped. 'Maybe he's had them killed, too?'

'I doubt it. That could cause problems with Kent. We don't know how he's connected. For them, this is purely business, remember? The fallout from the attack would be a setback, but their focus would be to limit the damage and carry on. Plus, everyone involved is literally invested in getting everything back on track.' He navigated to Google Maps on the laptop. 'There's no street view coverage of Navarro's Famara address, but it tallies with the couple's final phone mast ping, and it's in the area your waiter highlighted.'

Harley scooped out another glass. 'What if we're wrong, Jake?'

'About what?'

'About Kyle. We have to assume he's still alive. We should be having this conversation with Torres.'

He sighed. 'Like I said, I agree with Leona's instincts. If I were Navarro, I'd have someone inside Torres's department. Krueger has probably found out who we are already.'

Harley reeled. 'Fucking hell.' She scrambled to her feet and paced. 'Doesn't that *worry* you?'

Sawyer tossed a crust back into the carton, started on a new slice. 'Worrying about it won't help Kyle Goddard, if he is still alive.'

She peered at him, breathing hard. 'Jake, I feel sick. The picture we've painted of these people… They're *serious*. Rich. Powerful. Ruthless. They might feel they'd be safer if we weren't around. You don't have to impress me by pretending you're not scared.'

'I'm not pretending. Just trying to stay focused.'

'So, what the hell do we do?'

'We go with Plato. He said the virtuous life must follow four principles. Moderation…' He smiled, waved a hand across their simple spread. 'The others were justice—'

'That's what we're seeking for the couple.'

'Definitely. Also, wisdom…'

Harley moved in close again, sat on the tiles next to Sawyer. 'Okay. That works. That's what we've shown by putting all this together.' She studied him. 'And the fourth virtue?'

He shrugged. 'Courage.'

Chapter Nineteen

Sawyer steered the car off the tarmac onto a patch of scrub and cacti that thickened into a brittle rash as it sloped up to the base of the Risco de Famara cliff range.

'I don't think this is a road,' said Harley.

'It is now.'

He slowed to a crawl, hauling the car over the sandy earth, readjusting and rescuing it from wheelspin a couple of times. When they were a reasonable distance from the main road, he killed the engine and pointed at an isolated two-storey whitewashed house in the middle distance.

'Navarro's place?' said Harley.

Sawyer nodded, looked around. The mountains rolled down to the beach like a shovelling of grubby sand.

'I think this thing is thinning out,' he said.

'The *calima*? Maybe. The heat is still vile, though.' She turned to him, legs folded under her, then ducked down and looked up through the windscreen. 'How high are those cliffs?'

'Couple of thousand feet.'

'Bit much for what's basically a desert.'

He scrolled through something on his phone. 'Take it up with the original eruptions.'

'Jake. This is insane.'

'No, it's not. I just want to check an idea. If I were Navarro, I'd keep Hines and Wheeler where I could see them until I could ship them back to the UK. Maybe on fake ID. Plus, if Kyle is still alive, this is a good place to look.'

Harley flopped back in the seat. 'This is the part where I beg you to let me come with you, right? And you say no. You tell me to stay here. Tell me to raise the alarm if you don't come back in fifteen minutes. Maybe I secretly follow you and hit a bad guy with a chunk of cactus while he's holding a gun on you.'

'I'd say more like ten minutes.' Sawyer opened his door, smiled at her. 'So, is this real enough for you?' Harley turned away. 'Come if you like.'

'I don't like.' She waved an arm. 'Do what you need to do. Get what you think you need.'

'You know what that is.'

'What?'

'Evidence. Some sign the men are there. A concrete link to the attack on Fullerton and her boyfriend. I want to see a high-suspension car. Probably a Jeep. That would match with Leona's description. I mainly want Hines and Wheeler, though. We have their photos from London. We call it in to Torres and crew once we're sure. Otherwise, his team turn up and ask to look around, and Navarro can pull a classic stall for a warrant, move things around by the time they come back.'

Harley fumbled in the glovebox. 'So, this is like Section 17 in the UK?'

'That's one gold star each today. Yes. There must be an equivalent in Spanish law.'

She pulled out a handful of wine gums. 'Article 18 in the Spanish constitution. Section 2. *The home is inviolable. No entry or search may be made without the consent of the occupant or a legal warrant, except in cases of flagrante delicto.*'

'Isn't that a sex thing?'

'It's more of a caught-in-the-act thing. In this case, it refers to the process of committing a crime.' She slammed the glovebox closed with her foot and raised a finger. '*And…* Article 545 of the Criminal Procedure Act backs that up.' She picked out a black wine gum. 'I checked when you were in the shower. Jake…' She shuffled over to him, tilted her head forward and held firm eye contact. 'If you're doing this, you need a sugar hit.' She held up the sweet and he opened his mouth. 'But first. Please. No heroics. You see what you can see. You come back again.'

He nodded, and she slipped in the sweet, then handed him a bottle of water.

'The main question, though, is… would Plato approve? Is this really courage? Are you really out for justice? Is it bravery or bravado?'

He chewed, took a deep drink, then stepped out of the car. 'Let's switch philosopher. Marcus Aurelius. Roman Emperor. Stoic. The original and best. He said you can commit injustice by doing nothing.'

Chapter Twenty

Sawyer stayed low, using his phone light to navigate across the uneven scrubland. The sun had set, and, across the plain, the ocean twinkled under diffuse moonlight.

He stumbled, suppressing a constricted cough as he righted himself. The air was dense and gritty, and he formed a makeshift filter by pulling the neck of his T-shirt over his mouth and nose.

As he drew near to the house, sounds cut through the murk: shouts, a musical pulse.

He pushed on to the edge of a dirt track that ran alongside the house and merged with a steep rocky trail up and around the cliffside.

Splashes now, from a pool. Delighted shrieks: female. Lewd laughter: male.

He crossed the track and slipped into a narrow paved alley, staying close to a heavy-duty chain link fence around the perimeter, tracking the noise to the back side of the building.

The alley ended at a strip of open scrub that fell away

into unlit borderland. Visibility was poor, but he could just make out a village of modular rentals, perched on high ground above the beach.

Sawyer aimed his phone light across the ground and caught a silver Jeep Compass, tucked in behind an outbuilding. He edged closer, crouched at the foot of the fence, and took a photo of the car.

He kept still, listening to the buzz of the pool filter, close enough to muffle the shouts and splashes.

'The ladies are thirsty!' A male voice. British.

Female voices, chattering in Spanish.

Male voice again. *'Clint! Refills, if you will. And they need powder for their noses.'*

Female laughter.

Sawyer sent a message—and the picture—to Harley. He looked up and studied the outbuilding. It wasn't low enough to climb, but he could get to it from the car roof.

A sight of the pool would seal it. Maybe even a photo.

He would be invisible to the revellers back here, and they sounded distracted.

He pocketed the phone and crouch-walked to the Jeep.

A handgun cocked, in the alley behind. Then, a dark, self-satisfied laugh.

'Smile for the camera, culero. Get your fucking arms up in the air, nice and high, and don't turn around.'

Ruiz.

Sawyer raised his arms and looked up to the top of the fence.

'Not there, dickhead. Hands on the car. Lean forward. And don't worry. You're fucked enough as it is.'

More laughter.

Sawyer rested both palms on the car roof and lowered

his head. He squinted into the glass, looking for a glimpse of Ruiz's reflection.

But he covered the ground quickly.

A blunt weight slammed into the back of Sawyer's skull, jerking his forehead into the car roof.

He dropped hard, into the dirt.

Chapter Twenty-One

Sawyer woke to swirling sand, scattering through his hair, settling on his lips.

He spat and opened his eyes. He lay on his side, on warm earth, wrists tied and wrapped around his shins with duct tape. A muted pain thumped at the back of his head, sharpening as he came round.

'Rise and shine.' The enormous man Sawyer had met in Arrieta sat on the bonnet of the Jeep, parked against an outcrop of rock a few yards back from the cliff edge.

Sawyer hauled himself upright, and hot wind whipped his hair back.

'Nice to see you again.' The man hitched forward and climbed off the bonnet, raising the ride height considerably. A second man—smaller, older—climbed down from the passenger seat and closed the door behind him.

'The feeling isn't mutual.' Sawyer nodded at the big man. 'Hugo Krueger.' He studied the second man: white polo, navy chinos, tan loafers. 'David Navarro.' Sawyer leaned back against another outcrop. 'I'm honoured.

The brains trust. Who's looking after Travis and Clinton?'

Krueger's eyes shifted briefly to Navarro. 'Our Colombian friend.'

Sawyer looked at Navarro. 'Kind of you to bring in some entertainment for them. Must be a pain, looking after a pair of pet rapists.'

Krueger unsheathed a carving knife. The serrated blade flashed in the moonlight as he walked to the cliff edge and peered over. 'You did pretty well. I guess you came in on foot, off the road. Strange, though. Either you didn't think we'd have security, or you didn't care.' He turned. 'I did some homework on you, Detective Sawyer. You're way too smart to not assume we'd have security.'

'You cheated,' said Sawyer. 'You can't outsmart a hidden camera.'

Krueger smiled, waved the knife in the air. 'No, no. You know what I think? I think you actually didn't care. Like you have some sort of death wish.'

'And you're planning to fulfil it?'

Krueger walked to Sawyer, head down. 'Would it make any difference?' He crouched, a few feet away. 'You're here to help the police, but I wonder if they even know what you know. We couldn't get into your phone, but Ruiz said you were using it before he caught you.' Krueger dug the point of the blade into the dirt and scraped out a slow line. 'Calling in the cavalry?' He winced, shook his head. 'You don't strike me as a cavalry kind of guy.' He stood up, looked down at Sawyer. 'You've been through some shit, man. Your mother. Your brother... People don't come back from that. You should be stacking supermarket trolleys. Not taking on scumbags like me.'

'We have motion sensors,' said Navarro, stepping away from the Jeep. 'You came through to the back of the house. Maybe you took pictures. And you stuck around. Were you planning to break into my house? Alone? Did you skip your risk assessment course, Mr Sawyer? Or are we giving you too much credit? Maybe you're just plain stupid.'

Sawyer dug his head into his shoulder, sucked in a big breath. He turned and spat. A squall of wind swooped across the clifftop, stirring a vortex of sand and earth. He raised his eyes to Navarro. 'Where's Kyle Goddard? Tied up in your basement? Under the desert?' He nodded out to sea. 'Sleeping with the fishes? Did you really kill some anonymous guy for the sake of international relations?'

'Things got messy,' said Navarro. 'And now, you're part of the mess.'

Sawyer propped himself higher against the rock. 'So, that's your plan? Clean up? Carry on as if nothing happened?'

Navarro stepped closer. He pushed his fingers through his greying hair, slicking it back, then took out a handkerchief and wiped them down. He stood next to Krueger with his hands in his pockets, gazing down at Sawyer. 'Nothing *did* happen. For so long, we have no control. We sit by, while others write the story of our lives. Why else would we pursue money and power and status, Mr Sawyer, but for the ability to take control? To rewrite the story. Change the past. Make it unhappen.'

'The past isn't something set or over,' said Sawyer. 'It's all in motion.'

Navarro grinned. 'Have you read Pablo Neruda? My favourite poet.'

'I'm a Larkin man.'

He pointed. 'Never heard of him. Neruda... He speaks to the universal soul.'

Navarro nodded at Krueger. He gripped Sawyer by the back of his neck and dragged him through the dirt, out to the cliff edge, then yanked him upright, hand gripping his neck, tilting him forwards.

Sawyer looked down into the ocean, roiling far below. Spume foamed up along the shoreline; as it always had, as it always would.

'You have an interesting past, friend,' said Krueger. 'Your future, not so much.' He crouched next to Sawyer and pushed his head in close. 'I see you, Detective Sawyer. A good guy who likes to get close to the bad guys. Unloading his pain.' He tilted Sawyer further forward, dislodging a few rocks that tumbled over the edge. Sawyer kept his eyes open. Krueger's mouth was at his ear. 'And we know what happens when you stare into the abyss, right? Into the darkness.'

'In the long dark night of the soul,' said Navarro, 'it's always three in the morning.'

Sawyer kept his breathing steady. 'That's a misquote. Fitzgerald actually said, "the *real* dark night of the soul". But, as English is your second language, you get a pass.'

Navarro laughed and gave another sharp nod. Krueger yanked Sawyer away from the edge and dumped him back beside the rock. 'Okay, then. Back to native ground. Neruda. A Spanish speaker.'

Sawyer turned himself round to face Navarro. 'Chilean Spanish. Close enough.'

'Neruda said life is a constant process of discarding the past, so that each new day "gleams like an empty plate".' He paced, gesticulating as he quoted. 'There is nothing. There was always nothing. It all has to be filled with a new, expanding fruitfulness.'

Sawyer glanced at Krueger, standing with the knife at his side. 'I'll raise you a fellow countryman of mine. George Orwell. "Who controls the past controls the future. Who controls the present controls the past."'

Navarro waved a hand. 'Cynical. Orwell wasn't a poet. He was a glorified journalist.'

Sawyer hitched his back against the rock. 'I'd love to continue this discussion into literary matters. But can you just answer me one question?'

Navarro turned, gave him a slow nod. 'Be quick.'

'Is the Hulk going to stab me or push me off the cliff? I'm just wondering why the theatrics if he's got a fucking big knife.'

Krueger stooped and gripped Sawyer's arm, holding him steady. 'The knife is for you, yes.' He slipped it between the tape around Sawyer's wrist and sliced it away. 'What you did to Ruiz, friend…' He cut away the rest of the tape around Sawyer's legs and fixed him with probing grey eyes. 'It excited me, you know? I haven't had a two-sided fight in a long time.'

Sawyer slumped against the rock, rubbing his wrists to get the blood flowing.

Navarro walked back to the car, keeping his distance.

Krueger peeled off his T-shirt. 'We have a bag in the boot. Weights. You are going over the edge, Mr Sawyer. But first, I will have my sport.'

Sawyer rose to his feet, getting his bearing. He swiped sweat and sand from his brow. 'Could we leave it until the weather's cooled off a bit more?'

'Hugo!'

Navarro called from the car. Krueger stormed past

Sawyer and looked down the winding track that led up to the clifftop.

Sawyer climbed up onto the rock and saw the source of their alarm.

A line of two blue-and-white Policia Nacional cars sped up the narrow road, blue roof lights flashing.

'*Fuck!*' Krueger strode past Sawyer and hurled the knife over the cliff, into the water below. He crouched at the edge, gazing out to sea.

'Don't do it, Hugo,' said Sawyer, climbing down. 'Maybe they'll let us fight before they arrest you. Like you said, there's not much excitement here.'

The cars reached the top and a group of armed officers carrying MP5 submachine guns exited the lead car and fanned out across the entrance to the clifftop. The lead officer advanced, shouting to Navarro and Krueger in Spanish. They both raised their arms as three of the officers escorted them to the first car.

Torres got out of the second car and opened the back door. Harley exited and hurried over.

She stood off him, arms folded.

'You took photos of Hines and Wheeler from my laptop when I was in the shower,' said Sawyer. 'You spoke to Torres, and he called the hospital, got positive ID from Fullerton. You told him I thought I knew where the men were, and you'd let him know as soon as it was confirmed. I confirmed it, then you relayed the message to Torres with the address...' He held up a hand, thinking. 'And... you gave him our car's location and followed him when he passed the point we came off the main road.'

He caught his breath, sat down by the rock.

'Real policing,' she said, smiling.

Chapter Twenty-Two

TWO DAYS LATER

Harley pointed straight overhead. 'That's the Summer Triangle. Vega is the top point.'

Sawyer tipped back his head and looked through the binoculars, up into the night sky. A star blazed in line with Harley's finger.

She stood behind him, arms around his shoulders. 'It's the fifth brightest in the sky. Down to the left is Deneb, and over on the right is Altair.'

'It's a bluey white,' said Sawyer.

'I know. Isn't it beautiful? God, it's so clear up here. No light pollution. My brother used to take me to Blythe Hill Fields. It was okay, but this is *pure*. What else can you see?'

He studied the constellations inside the triangle, letting his eyes settle. 'There's a diamond.'

She grabbed the binoculars. 'Yes! Delphinus. Four stars with a little tail. This is insane, Jake. I think I can even see Vulpecula.' She looked at him, eyes wide. 'Only two stars and really dim. You can see it here, clear as…'

'Day?'

'Aren't you going to ask me the four brightest stars?'

'Are you going to tell me?'

She rehung the binoculars around her neck. 'No. Can't remember them all. I know Sirius is number one.'

'Everyone knows that.' Sawyer moved away from the small group of hikers and stargazers and glanced back to the orange Peñas del Chache observatory dome. Harley followed, and they sat at the edge of the walking trail, shielded from the wind by a cluster of rock.

'This is as far as we can go,' said Sawyer. He caught her eye. 'About two thousand two hundred feet above sea level.'

Harley cued up some music on her phone: a rumbling bass, sparse synth notes blending into a gauzy, cycling riff.

'*Équinoxe*,' he said.

'Yes! Jean-Michel Jarre. My brother insisted on playing it when we did our stargazing. It's grown on me over the years.'

'Breaks your 1980s-only policy, though.'

She sighed. 'It's not a policy.'

They looked out across the volcanic crags, tumbling down to Famara Bay.

'So, the 1980s thing is your brother's fault?'

She nodded. 'Before Nick died, he was into bands and weird electronic stuff. I was very little in the late 1980s, but the music got into my bones somehow. It wasn't just him, though. Mummy loved 1980s music, too. She liked the female singers. Have a guess who her favourite was. There's a big clue in my name.'

He thought for a moment. 'Madonna?'

She shoved him. 'I used to be teased constantly at school. You could say from nine to five.'

Sawyer laughed, gazed up at the sky.

They fell silent for a while.

'Will they find Kyle Goddard, Jake?'

'I doubt it. No body. No comment. And Krueger ditched what was probably the murder weapon into the sea. Torres has Wheeler and Hines's DNA from Leona, so there's a strong case for sexual assault. Aggravated, too…'

'Five to ten?'

He nodded. 'I might need to testify on Navarro and Krueger's kidnap charge. But it probably won't get to court. Navarro's lawyers will argue I was trespassing, and they took me from the house for the safety of their guests.'

'That's such bullshit.'

'Of course it is. They'll also throw Wheeler and Hines under the bus. Maybe arguing they came to the house with the girls. If we're right about the Kent and Navarro connection, Wheeler and Hines will take their medicine and keep quiet.'

She gave a muted laugh. 'Torres wasn't happy with you.'

'I know. That lecture in the car. About my actions putting others in danger.'

'Thing is, Jake. He's right. Isn't he?'

He shuffled around, facing her. 'We got the bad guys. Justice for Leona.'

'You could have died.'

'Could have. Didn't.'

She turned to him. 'Weren't you *scared?*'

He took a breath. 'No. I don't really… It just doesn't work on me like it seems to do with others. Fear. I'm not bragging. I just… don't get it. I don't feel it.'

She edged close, held his wrist. 'That's not a good thing. Fear keeps us safe. It keeps us alive. Not to have it…

That's more like a super-weakness than a superpower. And yes. It puts the people you care about in danger. Do you even realise how lucky you were the other night? You might not always have someone looking out for you.'

'Fullerton asked me if I was in therapy.'

'It's a good question.' She turned away. 'I lost my brother early, too, Jake. Not... like you did with your mum. We always knew Nick wasn't going to live long. Cystic fibrosis is a bitch, and they didn't have the drugs back then. So I had to grow up fast. I had to keep Mummy going. And Daddy. And I had a brilliant counsellor. He said that he didn't believe in *closure*. He didn't see grief as something that starts and ends. He said it doesn't stay put. It's always with you, all around you. Some days it's like a light breeze. Others, more of a hurricane. But you must develop strategies on how you respond to it.' Harley pivoted back to face him. 'Whatever happens with us, I hope you can find peace and take time to work on yourself, before you get into a situation where you don't have an overqualified Community Support Officer watching your back.'

He smiled. 'You'll be in Hatfield's chair before me.'

Harley lay back and stared up. Sawyer mirrored her, the back of his head bedding into the sun-baked ground.

She reached over, held his hand. 'So, what do you think death is like?'

'You do know how to milk a romantic moment.'

'I used to read Terry Pratchett books when I was a teenager. They were Nick's. I teased him for being a nerd, but I read them in secret. There's a bit in *Reaper Man* that hit me hard after he died. I underlined it in the book.'

Sawyer turned to her.

Harley winced. 'Yes, I know. It was only in pencil.

Anyway, in the story, there's a village where they believe no one is dead until the "ripples they cause in the world die away". The idea that the span of someone's life is only the core of their actual existence.'

Sawyer pondered for a moment. 'That's why we're here now. Ripples from your brother.'

'*Jake*. Don't!'

'Sorry. To answer your question… It's all in the stars. As I'm sure Nick told you, most of those lights up there began their journey to our retinas way before we were born. That's a big trip. A long dark journey from the cold depths of space to the light-receptive cells in our warm bodies. So, like the stars, we come from dark to light, and then go back to dark again. My mum used to say there was nothing in darkness that wouldn't be brought to light. The answers are out there somewhere, but they just haven't arrived yet.' He held a hand up to the sky. 'So, here we lie, staring at the past. You get told to not live there. To keep going forward. Don't look back. But for some people, the past is all they can see. It's their lifelong project, managing those ripples. A work in constant progress. Like your counsellor said, there's no such thing as closure.'

Harley sat up. 'And we recreate the past in the present all the time. Usually as a comfort thing. Our music. Memories.'

Sawyer stayed on his back. 'Yeah. I agree with Pratchett. The individual is just in a bad way physically at the moment of their death. They only truly *die* when their ripples fade away.' He raised himself up, leaning on Harley's shoulder. 'In the years after my mum died, I saw her a lot. In person. Usually in times of stress. I knew she wasn't *real*. It was like talking to myself in a mirror.

Working through things. But then that stopped, and I took it as a sign of healing. Now, I want it to happen again.'

'But you just said you knew it wasn't real.'

Sawyer looked up, into the night. 'If I can't be with her for real, then I'll settle for her ripples. And I can't bring her back, no. But I can find whoever took her away.'

Ready for the full DI Jake Sawyer series?

vinci-books.com/jakesawyerseries

Pacy and dark **police procedurals** set within the bleak beauty of the UK Peak District.

Part **murder mystery**, part **psychological thriller**. Twists, black humour, and a compelling lead character whose backstory develops through the series.

Addictive, page-turning stories from one of the UK's sharpest *writers. Perfect for fans of **Val McDermid**, **MJ Arlidge**, **Ian Rankin**, **LJ Ross**, and **Michael Connelly**.*

"Tightly plotted and superbly written."
⭐⭐⭐⭐⭐

"Dark and twisted, with genuine surprises."
⭐⭐⭐⭐⭐

"Well developed characters in a wonderful setting."
⭐⭐⭐⭐⭐

Next in the Jake Sawyer series

vinci-books.com/creepy

A killer who won't forgive. A detective who can't forget.

Haunted by his mother's brutal murder, Detective Inspector Jake Sawyer returns to his rural hometown to investigate a series of gruesome killings. As the body count rises and the killer's twisted methods come to light, Sawyer must confront his own demons while racing against time to unravel the shocking truth behind the murders.

With his sanity and safety on the line, Sawyer pushes himself to the brink to end the killings and save an innocent life.

An edge-of-your-seat page-turner that will keep you guessing to the very end.

CREEPY CRAWLY is Book one in the page-turning DI Jake Sawyer crime thrillers. Perfect for fans of Ian Rankin, Val McDermid, Chris Carter, and Karin Slaughter.

★★★★★ "A dark and twisted murder mystery with genuine surprises."

★★★★★ "The pace never lets up."

★★★★★ "I was holding my breath during the final scene."

★★★★★ "Well plotted and superbly written."

★★★★★ "Gripping."

★★★★★ "Well-developed characters in a wonderful setting."

★★★★★ "I'm in love with DI Sawyer."

★★★★★ "Awesome."

★★★★★ "Compelling."

★★★★★ "Dark and intense and worth every minute."

★★★★★ "I wish I hadn't read it, so I could read it for the first time again."

vinci-books.com/creepy

Printed in Great Britain
by Amazon